"You've stopp[...]
Joshua murm[...]

Riffy, wretched Riffy, lunged over Brogan's other shoulder and grabbed his hair.

"Dad, dad, dad," she shrieked gleefully, and Joshua lifted her across, held her easily in one arm, turned Brogan, drew her close and kissed her.

His mouth left hers slowly, reluctantly, and amusement shone in his eyes. "She's wet."

"What?"

"Your daughter." Soft, seductive eyes still holding hers, he repeated, "She's wet."

"Oh, right, yes, I mean…it's water, not…" With a ragged sigh she took her daughter back, shook her head defeatedly and walked out.

"Monkey," she muttered at her unrepentant daughter. "And that is not Daddy." Daddy hadn't looked in the least like Joshua. But then, Riffy never would see her daddy and so couldn't be blamed, she supposed, for thinking any man that came within her orbit might be him. Even Joshua.

READFUL THINGS
PAPERBACK EXCHANGE
741 SO. TAYLOR
FALLON, NV 89406
702 - 423-7875

Dear Reader,

This year is the fortieth anniversary of Harlequin Romance—an achievement unsurpassed in the world of romance fiction! Well, they say life begins at forty, and although my life didn't actually *begin* at forty (by then I had a husband and three beautiful little girls to prove it!), it certainly changed direction. I became a writer—and all because I couldn't find anything to read!

I'm generally amiable—well, you have to be when you have a husband who takes twenty-seven years to build the garage! Some things have changed over the years, however—my three little girls have grown into delightful women, and we now have three precious grandchildren. A constant source of inspiration!

They also say be careful what you wish for, you might get it. And so, nearly ten years and over twenty books later, I'm still careful but delighted to have got what I wished for and to be part of Harlequin's success story! And we owe it all to you—the readers! Thank you for reading my books over the years, and Happy Anniversary, Harlequin Romance!

With best wishes,

Emma Richmond

First-Time Father
Emma Richmond

Harlequin Books

TORONTO • NEW YORK • LONDON
AMSTERDAM • PARIS • SYDNEY • HAMBURG
STOCKHOLM • ATHENS • TOKYO • MILAN
MADRID • WARSAW • BUDAPEST • AUCKLAND

If you purchased this book without a cover you should be aware
that this book is stolen property. It was reported as "unsold and
destroyed" to the publisher, and neither the author nor the
publisher has received any payment for this "stripped book."

ISBN 0-373-03453-9

FIRST-TIME FATHER

First North American Publication 1997.

Copyright © 1996 by Emma Richmond.

All rights reserved. Except for use in any review, the reproduction or
utilization of this work in whole or in part in any form by any electronic,
mechanical or other means, now known or hereafter invented, including
xerography, photocopying and recording, or in any information storage
or retrieval system, is forbidden without the written permission of the
publisher, Harlequin Enterprises Limited, 225 Duncan Mill Road,
Don Mills, Ontario, Canada M3B 3K9.

All characters in this book have no existence outside the imagination of
the author and have no relation whatsoever to anyone bearing the same
name or names. They are not even distantly inspired by any individual
known or unknown to the author, and all incidents are pure invention.

This edition published by arrangement with Harlequin Books S.A.

® and TM are trademarks of the publisher. Trademarks indicated with
® are registered in the United States Patent and Trademark Office, the
Canadian Trade Marks Office and in other countries.

Printed in U.S.A.

PROLOGUE

'THE Church of SS Peter and Paul in front of you is one of the highest in East Ang—'

Breaking off, aware of a small disturbance behind her, aware of the accelerated beat of her heart, positively *knowing* who it would be, Brogan slowly turned as a tall, dark-haired man joined the group. He made no apology for his lateness, made no remarks at all, merely stared at her with eyes that looked almost black. Cold, unemotional, he had a sternly forbidding countenance, until he gave that maddening half-smile and raised one eyebrow, as though they were—intimate. Which they weren't. She didn't know him at *all*!

He'd been following the tour for two days now, made it blatantly obvious that he was only following it because of her, and she didn't know *why*! Alarmed by his interest, disturbed by the attraction she felt for this austere-looking man, the bewilderment in her large grey eyes turned to embarrassment. She'd even been *dreaming* about him, for goodness' sake! And anticipating his arrival.

Swinging hastily back to the group, his image still clearly imprinted on her retina—denim shirt, denim jeans, and the haversack he always carried—she gave a lame smile, pushed curly brown hair off a damp forehead. 'Sorry, where was I? Oh, yes.' Flustered, befuddled, almost able to *feel* his eyes on her, she continued with a desperation that should have been comical, and wasn't. 'The families of de Vere and Spring made the church the landmark it is today, with the tower at a hundred and forty feet hi—'

'One,' a languid voice in the vicinity of her left ear informed her.

Wrenching round again, forced to take a step back, she demanded blankly, 'What?'

'A hundred and forty-*one* feet,' he murmured helpfully.

'Oh. Right. You'd like to take the tour, would you?'

He shook his head, smiled, but not with his eyes. And brown eyes were never meant to be that cold, she thought distractedly; she hadn't believed they ever could be, until now.

Despite his obvious interest in her, as inexplicable as *that* might be, and despite his lazy amusement, his eyes never warmed, and that both attracted and repelled. There was no warmth in that stern face, despite the half-smile, nothing to latch onto, nothing to indicate that he was this sort of person or that. He was a watcher, a man on the outside, looking in. Not wistfully, not yearningly, but because he didn't want to be a part of the whole.

'And also noted for its fine woodwork,' he added in obvious amusement. 'Joshua Baynard,' he introduced himself softly.

Mesmerised by eyes that held a frightening intensity, by a stern face and a half-smile that wasn't any sort of smile at all, she had to be prompted into giving her own name by the lift of one eyebrow;

at least, she had thought that was what he was prompting.

'Brogan. Yes, it's Brogan. Brogan—'

'I know,' he interrupted.

Yes, of course he did. She always introduced herself to the group. Always gave her name. But he hadn't given his, hadn't spoken, until now. And that voice. Oh, dear God, that voice. Seductive, warm. It prompted a desire to be—wanton, made promises of things to come.

Feeling a fool, feeling threatened, she found it impossible to ignore him, to tell him to leave her alone. Emotions she'd thought gone, buried, were resurfacing at an alarming rate. He heightened senses she hadn't known she had, heightened perception. 'I have to—'

'Tour the village, yes.'

Snapping her eyes away, feeling stupid and inadequate, feeling lost, breathless, almost frightened, she searched frantically for her group, found them examining the outside of the church, commenting on the carving, and prayed they wouldn't ask her questions on it, clapped her hands to gain their attention, and was aware—so very aware—that he still watched her.

Joshua. Joshua Baynard. Giving him a nervous smile, a flicker of bewilderment, she shepherded her group back to the road, began leading them along the high street, past the crazy angles of half-timbered houses, and explained the meanings of the trade marks, carvings and family emblems on the hall houses and cottages. A warm finger touched her neck, and she halted, gulped, shivered, hurried to get away.

They reached the guildhall almost at a run. Breaking into speech, she gabbled through its history, and because she had learned it by rote, because she was only filling in for the usual tour guide, she needed to say it all, otherwise she tended to forget where she'd got to.

'And after the collapse of the wool industry the guildhall became a prison and later a workhouse. If you would like to go inside, there are displays about the wool industry, and also further information on Lavenham.'

The group moved inside, and Brogan let out a long sigh of relief, leaned against the wall, only to leap upright again when a seductive voice enquired lazily, 'A cold drink?'

Swinging round, she stared at him in despair. 'What?' she asked huskily.

'I thought we might have a drink whilst we wait. You look hot.'

'No. I mean, it's a hot day... Don't you want to see inside the guildhall?'

'No.' Reaching out, he traced a finger along her lower lip and she jumped back in shock.

'What are you *doing*?'

'Touching you.'

'Well, don't! You mustn't! You don't know me!'

'But want to,' he said softly.

'Look...' she began desperately.

'Mmm?'

'Stop it! Why are you *doing* this?'

'Because I think you're the most beautiful young woman I've ever seen.'

'Most beautiful?' she echoed faintly. 'Don't be absurd; I'm not in the *least* beautiful.'

'Aren't you?' he queried lazily.

'No!'

He took her left hand, raised it, examined the wedding band that circled her finger, stared into her eyes, and waited.

Struck dumb, sensible enough to know that she should tell him nothing, Brogan just stared at him. She didn't think he was *dangerous* exactly, but he frightened her in a way she'd never been frightened before. Sexually frightened. She was also vulnerable. Widowed with a small baby, she *had* to be sensible. 'Who are you?' she whispered.

'I told you.'

'No—no, you didn't—just your name.'

He smiled that fascinating half-smile, and gave an explanation that explained nothing. 'I have an interest in architecture.'

'Then why are you doing this to *me*?'

'Because you're—interesting.'

'I don't want to be interesting!' Snatching her hand away, she stared desperately at the entrance to the guildhall, prayed her group would appear.

'When do you finish shepherding the flock?'

'Why?' she demanded huskily.

'Because I intend to take you home.'

'No!'

'Yes.'

'No,' she denied worriedly. Men never pursued her... Why would men pursue her? she wondered frantically. 'I don't have any money... Why are you laughing? Don't laugh! It isn't funny!'

'No,' he agreed lazily, 'I don't suppose it is. What else is there to see?'

'You know what there is to see! You've been following me for *days*!'

'So I have. The Priory, the Wool Hall, The Old Grammar School, the de Vere House and Shilling Grange,' he enunciated softly. 'Where Jane Taylor lived. The Jane Taylor who wrote "Twinkle, Twinkle, Little Star"—and how I wonder what *you* are,' he added softly. So very, very softly.

Confused, she opened her mouth, closed it again, desperately tried to pull herself together as her group appeared. With a smile that felt plastic, she led them off on the rest of the tour with no clear idea afterwards what she had said or done. She only knew that the man with brown eyes was—interested. Made her feel a fool. She was afraid for the tour to end, afraid to be alone with him, because this time, she *knew*, he would not walk away with the rest of the group. *This* time it would be different.

Frantically seeking excuses in her mind, she was then cross with herself. She didn't need to make excuses, just to tell him to push off, that she wasn't interested. But she was—and so very ill equipped to deal with it.

Her smile fixed, she thanked the group for their patience with her, hoped they would enjoy the rest of their stay, and, so very conscious that Joshua stood close behind her, almost able to feel the warmth of his body, she stayed stiffly still. Waited.

And when the waiting went on too long—far too long—she said stiltedly, 'I have to go now.'

'Good,' he said softly. 'Where shall we go?'

'*I*,' she stated clearly. 'Not we!'

He touched her shoulder, turned her, looked down into her worried face, and his smile was—electrifying. Tangling his fingers in hers, his eyes never once leaving her face, he tugged her away from the tourist office. 'This way?'

'Yes. No. You can't come with me!'

'Why? Hubby might object?'

'No! I don't...' Biting her lip, she turned her face away, tried to remove her fingers from his.

'Don't have a hubby?'

Mutinously silent, she dragged her hand away, determinedly faced him, opened her mouth—and he put one long finger across her lips.

'People have to meet somewhere, some time. A man sees a woman he likes, is fascinated by... A woman sees a man...'

'No.'

'Yes. And there's no need to look worried, frightened. I don't intend you harm, only to find out about you, learn your—history.' He smiled. 'So, where shall we go?'

'I have to pick up Riffy.'

'Riffy?'

'My daughter.'

'How old is she?'

'One—nearly one,' she qualified. 'And *I* will go and pick her up, not *we!*' Worry and confusion in her lovely eyes, she stared helplessly at him, tried to instil some firmness into her voice. 'I'm very flattered,' she added stiltedly, 'but I really don't want any involvement at the moment. I'm sorry.'

Dragging her eyes from his, she hurried away, prayed he wouldn't follow her. Heart beating over-fast, she scooted round the corner, hastily collected her daughter from the woman who had looked after her whilst she took the tour, mumbled some inane excuse about not stopping and having to get home, opened her car which was parked there, and quickly fitted Riffy into her car seat.

'Boddee!'

With a splutter of laughter, Brogan tucked her daughter's dress back over her bare tummy, gently removed the little hands that were about to yank it up again, and firmly fitted the seat belt. 'Yes, I know it's a body, but we have to go home now—'

Breaking off, feeling a definite *prickle* on the back of her neck, she watched Riffy glance behind her, purse her lips in a comical little parody of a kiss, and swung round. Crouched so that his eyes were on a level with her daughter's, Joshua gave a slow smile.

'Go away!'

'Dad, Dad, Dad!' Riffy shrieked.

'It isn't Dad,' she denied automatically as she backed carefully out and slowly stood. 'I said no,' she told Joshua in as neutral a tone as she could manage, but her heart was beating over-fast and there was a little sick feeling in her stomach.

'I didn't believe you.'

Without answering, she shut the back door, caught her foot in the strap of his rucksack which sat at his feet, muttered, cursed, pushed him away when he tried to help, and could have cried.

'Sorry,' he murmured. 'All my worldly possessions.'

Not caring, not believing him, just wanting to *go*, she thrust herself into the car and locked the door. With a hand that shook, she fired the engine and took off. Flicking her eyes to the rear-view mirror, she saw Joshua standing where she had left him. Blue jeans and an enigmatic smile. And with the brief glance she afforded him before dragging her eyes away she decided that he looked—intimidating. With a little shiver, she drove quickly home.

Why was he doing this? She *wasn't* the sort of woman men pursued. And if he only knew the *half* of it, she thought with a bleak smile, he would run the proverbial mile. Her life was a mess, and likely to get messier. But if... No, she denied firmly. No ifs! She couldn't afford any more entanglements. Not financially, not emotionally!

Turning off onto a narrow lane and through high gate-posts minus the gates, she drove along the rutted drive towards her house. It was an old house—very old—with a charming air of neglect. Not the neglect of indifference, but the neglect of 'we weren't quite sure what to do with it, so we left it alone'. And it would continue to be left alone, she thought despairingly, because she had neither the time nor the money to do anything else.

Andrew's dream—restore it, refurbish it, then sell, start all over again. Only, there would not be an 'again' because her husband was dead. If she sold, even if she *could* sell, it would be at a loss and then she wouldn't be able to afford anything else. It had taken all their savings to buy it. Andrew was to have restored it; she was to have done the interior. A business partnership, a good team. Should have been. Maybe she could turn it into a bed and breakfast, play up the old-world charm and hope no one would notice the dilapidation.

With a long sigh, she unclipped her daughter and carried her inside. To blissful quiet. A temporary quiet because in a few days Daniel would be back—Daniel who shared the house with her, Daniel who needed her. And if it weren't for Daniel . . .

No, that was foolish; even if there hadn't been Daniel to worry about, she didn't think she could afford to get involved with Joshua Baynard. Joshua Baynard looked—dangerous, and more troubles she certainly didn't need. He'd also looked as though he might be hard up, and hard up she didn't need!

She gave Riffy her tea, bathed her, put her to bed, but his image was still there, remained in her mind, and if there was a momentary wistfulness about her it was soon firmly dismissed.

Promising herself a five-minute read of the paper before she began on the numerous tasks that always seemed to be waiting, Brogan had just settled down when someone knocked on the door. No one ever knocked on her door. The few friends she had came round the back. So, it wasn't a friend.

Putting the paper aside, and with a feeling of trepidation, she walked slowly to open the front door—and found Joshua on her doorstep.

'I'm not so easily dismissed,' he stated quietly.

'I don't *want* you here.'

'Why?'

'Because... I don't have to have a *reason*!' she exclaimed in despair.

'Yes, you do. Can I come in?'

'No.'

He gave that fascinating little half-smile, took the door out of her hand and came in anyway. 'I'm not a rapist, a murderer or a thief. I merely want to get to know you better.' He produced a bottle of wine from behind his back and held it out for inspection.

'I don't drink,' she denied mutinously and quite untruthfully.

'Then keep it for a special occasion. Humour me,' he added softly.

Humour him? To what end? 'Who told you where I lived?'

'No one.' Indicating the battered car that stood beside her own, he explained simply, 'I followed you.'

'*Followed* me?' she shrieked in dismay.

'Mmm. I then went to have something to eat, bought the wine and returned. Why the ramp?' He was staring out of the window.

'What?'

'The door at the end of the annexe has a ramp fitted,' he explained patiently, as though she might not have known, as though it might have been fitted in her absence.

'I know. It's for the wheelchair. Daniel's wheelchair!' she added with a snap when he didn't answer. The wheelchair she had put him in—not intentionally, not deliberately, but had put him in nonetheless.

'Daniel?'

'He shares the house.'

'A lover?'

'No!' Red-faced, irritable, feeling wrong-footed, she glared at him, then away. 'He's a friend. Was a friend of my husband.'

'Ah. Coffee?'

Wanting to refuse, wanting him to go, she found herself leading the way to the kitchen, helpless in the face of his obduracy. Feeling stupid and inadequate, she busied herself putting the kettle on.

'What happened to him?'

'Who?'

'Daniel,' he replied with the same monumental patience.

'I did,' she said shortly. 'A wet road, a dark night, an unfamiliar car. Daniel had been drinking and so I offered to drive.' Had insisted, she remembered, and now she was held accountable. They had *all* held her accountable—the police, the ambulance crew—because, emotional and hysterical after the accident, Daniel had accused her, told them she had been driving too fast. But she hadn't; she'd been driving carefully—she always drove carefully.

She'd been guilty maybe of *misjudgement*, of overreacting, pulling too hard on the wheel when that motorbike had come out of nowhere—a motorbike Daniel hadn't seen, or said he hadn't— but there had been no proof of speeding, the measurement of skid marks had not produced any startling evidence, and so she had been let off with a warning—and the need to atone. She felt guilty and wretched, but she hadn't been driving too fast. All other considerations aside, Riffy had been in the car, and she would never, *never* put her daughter's life at risk.

'If the steep bank hadn't been there,' she resumed quietly, 'or the tree—if I'd swerved the other way, if I'd been used to power-assisted steering . . . But I wasn't, and the car mounted the bank, hit the tree and rolled back onto the road.'

She'd come out of it without a scratch, as had Riffy, strapped in her baby seat in the back, but Daniel had damaged his spine; she *still* didn't know how badly. Daniel said he would be in a wheelchair for life, but Daniel was a tense and nervous young man, prone to histrionics, so she didn't know if that was true.

Unaware she'd only half explained, she made the coffee and passed Joshua his cup.

'Where is he now?'

'Away for a few days finalising his collection. He's in fashion design.'

He nodded, continued to stare from the back window. 'What's that?'

Glancing at where he looked, she pulled a face. 'The cottage. I was thinking of doing it up, renting it out.'

He merely nodded again and turned to face her. Leaning his hips against the window-sill, he examined her face, gave that half-smile. 'How long have you been a widow?'

'Twenty months.'

'And how did your husband die?'

'He drowned,' she said bluntly. 'Surfing in a sea that was too rough.' And if he'd followed the advice he'd given everyone else—to check the tides, check with the coastguard, the locals... But he hadn't, and so he had died. No need to tell Joshua that; it was none of his business.

'Tough for you.'

'Yes.' No sympathy, no expressions of sorrow... Not that she wanted them. But still, it was odd for him to be so blunt. Odd for him to have asked. Most people didn't, avoided the subject like the plague, as though death might be catching, or she would crumple into a heap and embarrass both herself and them. Unaware of the rather defiant glitter in her eyes, she forced herself to stare at him. 'And you?'

'Unmarried.'

'And?'

Amused, he gave that half-smile, raised his left eyebrow. 'And what?'

'And what else are you?'

'An historical architect. I came to Suffolk in the hope of helping to rebuild an old Norman keep.'

'Oh.'

'And found myself attracted to a lady with big grey eyes instead.'

'Yes, well,' she mumbled awkwardly, 'I don't want you to be attracted, so I think you'd better go.'

He smiled again, put his cup on the table—and advanced. Brogan backed, eyes wide, wary. And when she had backed as far as she could, had been brought up short against a kitchen unit, he stood in front of her, gently removed her cup from her hand, placed it behind her, and rested one arm either side of her. Close enough for his thighs to brush hers, his arms to touch hers, he bent his head and kissed her—softly, surely, thoroughly, and with a great deal of expertise.

Shaking, worried, bemused, she stared at him mutely, hands clenched at her sides. The touch of his thighs against hers aroused feelings she fought to suppress; the shape of his mouth invited a touch she refused to bestow, a yearning she denied. And so, when she said nothing, *could* say nothing, he moved one hand, used long fingers to part her mouth, a thumb to rub seductively against her lower lip, an index finger to roll it down.

'No,' she groaned thickly.

'Yes.'

Eyes on his task, he bent his head again to kiss the inner surface of her lip, held her when she shuddered.

'Reciprocation's nice,' he prompted throatily.

'No,' she denied helplessly.

'Yes.'

'I *can't*!' she wailed.

'Why?'

'Because...' she began helplessly. 'Because it feels *wrong*!'

'In what way?'

'I don't *know*!'

Gathering her against him, he stared down into wide grey eyes, searched them for what felt like an eternity, and then he smiled, released her, kissed her nose. 'Goodnight,' he said softly. 'I can't come tomorrow.'

'I don't want you to come tomorrow.'

'But I'll be here the day after tomorrow.'

'*I* won't! I promised Daniel I'd help with his show!'

'Then I'll find you.' The half-smile flickered, and he was gone, the front door closing very quietly behind him.

Slumped where he had left her, she tried to make sense of something senseless. A man who could seduce without effort, without thought? She didn't think she had ever met anyone like him in her life! Didn't know how to behave with him. Didn't know what to *do*. And he could have been *anybody*! She'd let him into her house... Fool, Brogan.

The next day was spent in an agony of suspense. But he didn't come, as he had said he wouldn't. And early the following morning she drove to London, to Daniel, who needed her. And she didn't think that she had ever felt so disorientated, so confused in all her life.

CHAPTER ONE

'PAT-A-CAKE, pat-a-cake, baker—'

'Brogan!'

She sighed. 'Sorry.'

'You're here for *me*!'

'Yes, but Riffy likes—'

'Don't call her that! It's Poryphia!'

'I know it's Poryphia,' she agreed mildly. 'I named her. But it's such a long name for a little girl. Isn't it, sweetheart? That's it,' she encouraged Riffy warmly as the baby clapped her hands. 'Pat-a-cake, pat-a—'

'Brogan,' Daniel warned, ominously close to losing his temper. 'Don't.'

'Calm down,' she soothed. 'Everything's fine.'

'It is *not* fine! I should have gone for frivolity. I should—'

'Daniel...'

'Oh, damn you,' he cried despairingly. 'What do you know?'

'Enough to know that you're panicking unnecessarily.' Hefting the baby into a more comfortable position, she laid a gentle hand on Daniel's shoulder. 'You have the best spot, you have a good collection, the hall's full, the Press are here... Top *designers* are here. It will be fine. Trust me.'

'*Trust* you?' he asked bitterly. 'Yeah, look where *trusting* you got me!' Irritably shrugging her hand away, he rolled himself towards the clothes racks, began fingering his collection for the umpteenth time, and Brogan sighed defeatedly, gently removing the tiny hand that was exploring her mouth. Grey eyes bleak, she continued to watch the young man in the wheelchair. It was becoming grievously hard trying to atone for that one error of judgement.

Riffy jerked on her hair, and Brogan blinked, smiled, wrinkled her nose—and she was in the way, she finally realised.

'In your own time, dear.'

With a wry smile, she stepped out of the way of the harassed-looking model, and received a sarcastic, 'Thank you.'

Ho hum. Searching for a clear space where she *wouldn't* be in the way, she turned, blinked in disbelief, and froze, because the man who could turn her to jelly with just one look, turn her bones to water with just one touch was leaning indolently against the far wall. The man who shouldn't *be* here!

Languid, at ease, he gave that half-smile that was so electrifying, and raised one eyebrow—the eyebrow he always lifted. He could hold whole conversations with that damned eyebrow! Feeling threatened, nervous, *stupid*, she hurried across, asked worriedly, 'What are you doing here?'

'Watching you,' he murmured lazily as he extended one finger for the baby to grab.

Flushing, glancing quickly round, she whispered agitatedly, 'You aren't supposed to *be* here!'

'Going to snitch?'

Lazy amusement laced his voice, and she found it so very hard to cope. 'Don't be absurd.'

Remembering that kiss, she flushed, felt— wanton. She knew nothing about him except his interest in architecture—didn't want to know any- thing, she told herself. Just trying to cope with her feelings for this enigmatic man took all her energy. He made her feel vulnerable and aching, excited. All the yearnings she had ever had were now centred in one spot. And it wouldn't *do*! She had told herself and told herself on the long drive down that she wouldn't see him again, and that if she did she would tell him *straight*, honestly...

'You shouldn't be here,' she said weakly.

'Why?' he asked softly.

'Because you weren't invited, and because...' Because their meetings felt illicit; only, of course, they weren't; they felt like cheating, and weren't that either. She wished they had never met, wished she could stop thinking about him, stop feeling so worried and confused. Wished...

He was watching Daniel and she tried to see if there was accusation on his face, visible judgement, and saw none. His face, as always, remained—in- scrutable. His arms remained folded across his chest, distorting the line of his dark grey shirt; his ankles were crossed, his dark hair brushing the wall behind him. Attractive and insular, a man of great impact. His eyes moved to hers, and that faint, elusive smile tugged at his mouth, and she looked hastily away, defensive, threatened, feeling something jump inside.

'Brogan!'

With a little start, she hurried across to Daniel's side, was aware that Joshua watched.

'She won't wear it!'

'What?'

'The model,' he said crossly, as though she should have known immediately what he was talking about. 'She won't wear one of the outfits!'

'But she has to! She's a model, paid to do so!'

'Well, she won't. *Now* what do I do?'

'Which one is it?'

'It won't do any good!' he stated savagely. 'Even your famous diplomacy won't work this time! *You'll* have to do it! I'll hold the baby.' Reaching for her daughter, as he so often reached for her, he hugged Riffy, buried his face in her warm little neck, and Brogan wanted to warn him, Don't smother her; don't use her as your safety net. But how could she when the feel of Riffy's warm little body seemed to help him, calm him? And, truth to tell, Riffy didn't seem to mind, was gurgling with laughter in fact, tugging his fair hair.

Raising his head, he gave her a challenging look. 'You'll have to do it,' he repeated.

'Don't be daft. I'm not a model.'

'You're the right shape—long legs, no bust.'

'Don't be nasty. And I do have a bust. Not much, admittedly, but certainly a bust,' she added aggrievedly.

'Oh, to hell with it,' he muttered moodily. 'I don't even care. I'm going home.'

'Don't be ridiculous! You can't abandon it! You've worked hard for this. Where's the head of your college? Surely he can sort it out?'

'He's out front, buttering up the Press. And who *is* that?' he demanded as he glared at Joshua. 'Every time I turn round, he's staring!'

'Joshua Baynard,' she confessed reluctantly. 'He's a—friend.' Some friend, she thought hollowly. Friends aren't supposed to terrify you to death.

'Since when?' he asked suspiciously. '*I've* never seen him before.'

'So? You don't own me, Daniel. I am allowed friends.'

'Well, I don't like him!'

'Don't be childish.'

'Well, what do you expect? The collection's all wrong, and *you* won't help!'

'I'm not a model,' Brogan repeated numbly.

'It's not *much* to ask! You said you'd help...'

'I know, but not to *model*!'

'And God knows this is all your damned fault! Without you...'

Turning away, she closed her eyes in defeat. 'Which outfit is it?' she asked quietly.

'The black rubber.'

It would be. Oh, it would be. 'How long before your stuff's shown?'

'It not *stuff*!'

'Designs, then. How long?'

'About half an hour.'

Nodding, she sighed. 'Hang onto Riffy, otherwise she'll disappear. She does more disappearing acts than Houdini.' Walking across to the rails that held the senior students' collections, she managed to collar the model he'd pointed out as the one who'd refused to wear his design and asked her why.

'Because A,' the girl enunciated coldly as she shucked off one outfit and reached for another, 'it's too tight. B it's too hot, and C—' obviously the clincher '—I wouldn't have time to get into it or out of it. In case you hadn't noticed, he isn't the *only* one who needs my services.'

High heels and a thong, Brogan thought as the model unembarrassedly hurried back towards the curtain dividing the changing area from the main hall, dragging on the next outfit as she went. *All* the models stripped and changed without a thought—or care—for who might be watching. Naked breasts, naked bottoms...

Well, *she* wasn't a model, and *she* had no intention of stripping off, especially in front of Joshua. Grabbing the outfit, she walked behind the rail. And she was *definitely* keeping her knickers on!

Heaving and cursing, she finally managed to wriggle her hips into it, then gave herself a few seconds' breather before trying to fight her arms into the long, tight rubber sleeves.

'Talcum powder,' a laconic voice informed her.

Swinging round too quickly, she glared at Joshua, then hastily crossed her arms over her naked breasts. 'I don't have any talcum powder, and go away!'

He raised an eyebrow, glanced down, and observed with seemingly utter indifference, 'Spoils the line.'

'*What* spoils the line?'

He reached out and touched the slightly raised line that her panties made.

Jerking back, she gritted, 'I don't care! I am *not* taking them off!'

That small smile touched his mouth, quirked his lower lip. 'Pity.'

'And if you tell me,' she continued through her teeth, 'that I *owe* him my best shot I will probably become extremely violent!' She would take this emotional blackmail from Daniel—just—because she felt guilty, but she would not, positively not, take it from this cold, cynical stranger, who, for whatever reason, was taking an interest in something that was not his concern—taking an interest in a woman she would not have thought his type.

'And do you owe him?' he asked softly. 'Turn round.'

'What?'

'Turn round.'

With a last glare, she presented him with her back, felt him reach out, take hold of the outfit, and she stiffened, held herself very still, wanted to turn, *yearned* to, wanted to be held, and she didn't *know* him, *understand* him, and having him here, in her *other* life, seemed—wrong.

'Arm.'

Her face troubled, she shot out one arm. He clasped her wrist, pulled it backwards and began to ease it into the black rubber sleeve.

'Other one.'

Shooting out the other one, she allowed him to repeat the process. And he made the simple little operation seem—erotic. Nothing was said, nothing done, but it still felt seductive.

Grasping the back of the collar, he heaved and ordered mildly, 'Wriggle.' She wriggled, managed to get her shoulders in, and before she could protest he swung her round to face him, gave that odd little smile, and gently moved her breasts inside, allowing his fingers to linger. And she dragged in a sharp breath, stared at him with the eyes of a fool as he zipped her up.

Immobilised, arms stuck out sideways, hating him, wanting him, she was unable to do anything about the soft kiss he dropped on her mouth.

'Don't,' she urged, her voice husky, strangled, and wasn't sure which was worse—his electrifying presence or the tight, encasing rubber that made her feel stifled, panicky, claustrophobic. She could feel perspiration beginning to slide down her back, between her breasts, tried to take a deep breath and found she couldn't.

'Can you move?' He sounded hatefully amused.

She shook her head.

'Try.'

Giving him a look of dislike, she swung one leg forward and winced as the material cut into her groin. 'It's cutting off my circulation,' she protested. 'I'll never get to the *curtain*, let alone onto the catwalk...'

And that's when it hit her. She had to go down the catwalk. In front of all those people. Grabbing the zip, she attempted to yank it down; one long-fingered hand stopped her.

'I can't do this!'

'Yes, you can.' He picked up the headgear, which looked for all the world like a colander with a terminal disease, and put it on her head.

Oh, God.

'Walk.'

'I can't!'

'Walk.'

He was immune, immovable. He didn't raise his voice, didn't threaten; he didn't need to. She was Trilby to his Svengali. She couldn't take a deep breath—the outfit wouldn't allow it, would only allow shallow little pants. Defiance wasn't an option. You couldn't be defiant when you were being crushed to death.

Panic held barely in check, feeling sick, moving like a robot, she made her way out from behind the rail. Riffy chortled with delight, jumped up and down between Daniel's supporting hands.

'Glide,' Daniel ordered angrily. 'It's fluid, it's—'

'Daniel,' she interrupted. 'Have you ever worn this?'

'Of course I haven't.'

'Then don't tell me it's fluid! And as for gliding...'

Glaring at Joshua, he stated angrily, 'You didn't have to help her! And why has she got knickers on? I specifically said no knickers! And her hair! Look at it! I said no hair!'

'I am not shaving my head!'

Unflurried, unbothered, Joshua removed the helmet, dragged her long brown hair back, forced it into the collar of the suit, and put the helmet back. 'Glide.'

Models came and went, music blared, and, despairing, hot, feeling sick and numb because she was beginning to lose all feeling in her arms and legs, Brogan practised her glide. And if anyone could be said to hate then it was Brogan. And then Daniel's designated models came in, stripped off and began putting on his outfits. One glanced at Brogan, sniggered, and the hate was transferred to her. She was blonde and pouting, pretty and thin, and if Brogan had been able to move her arms she thought she would have hit her.

'Go last,' Daniel instructed. 'Do what they do.'

She just looked at him, her grey eyes promising retribution, and then remembered why she was here at the Banqueting House in the first place, and looked away.

It was guilt that had brought her and guilt that would make her model an outfit in this prestigious fashion and textile design show, held so that the senior students of the college could present a range of the ideas that they'd been working on throughout their course. It was supposed to be a celebration, not a wake, but because of her, because of the accident, there were only five outfits to be shown instead of the six there should have been. Could she really allow only four to be shown? No. It was just unfortunate that Daniel seemed to be into bondage.

'Go!' he urged hoarsely, and with no time left
to think she waddled after the other models, feeling
like a fool.

How she got down the catwalk she would never
know. Eyes fixed on nothing, peripherally aware of
the applause, the exclamations, the lights, heat,
flash bulbs, unable to glide fast, unable to keep up
with the other models and knowing that if she tried
she would probably fall over, she inadvertently gave
Daniel the one thing every student yearned for.
Time. A long time—for every member of the
audience to admire or disparage an outfit that
looked as though it might have been made for an
enemy of Captain Scarlet.

Deaf, blind, breathless and uncomfortable, she
shuffled off, tried to yank down the zip to give
herself room to breathe, and didn't even care that
it was Joshua who helped her, Joshua who exposed
her breasts as he dragged the top down over her
arms, pulled each hand free, dried her back, then
handed her the towel.

Holding it protectively against her, eyes closed,
dragging glorious breaths into her depleted lungs,
she vowed that no matter how desperate her straits
might be, and sometimes they were very desperate,
never, ever would she contemplate becoming a
model.

'Well done!' Daniel exclaimed, and for the first
time in weeks he sounded happy, animated. 'Oh,
Brogan, well done!'

Opening her eyes, she stared down at him, at her
chortling daughter, and managed a faint smile.

'Don't ever,' she warned him softly, 'ask me to do that again.'

'But you were brilliant! They're all furious that I got extra time!'

'Only because I couldn't walk any quicker! And please, please let me get out of this—bondage!' Removing the helmet, she hobbled over to the rail, dragged the outfit down to her ankles and thankfully stepped out of it. Hitching up her pants, wishing she could have a shower, she towelled herself dry then slipped into her print silk dress. It clung rather uncomfortably to her damp skin.

Sliding her feet into her tan sandals, she picked up the black rubber outfit and hung it back on the rail. She felt exhausted. And why did they have to hold the show in June? A very hot June at that. Why not in the autumn, when it would be cooler?

Fluffing out the damp ends of her hair, she sighed, wished with all her heart that she could go home. But she had promised to see it through to the end, and that meant waiting around whilst everybody congratulated everybody else, waiting whilst they had a drink to celebrate. Then there would be the long drive back to Suffolk.

Returning to the others, she reached for her daughter only to have Daniel shake his head, hold her tighter. 'She's all right with me.'

'Daniel—'

'Don't make a fuss,' he muttered. 'She likes being with me.' Before she could answer, before she could comment, he wheeled himself away to talk to someone and Brogan watched him helplessly. It was getting worse—this proprietorial attitude he had towards her daughter. Worse, and extremely worrying.

He behaved as though Riffy were his, allowed people to assume she was and that Brogan was more than just a friend—and that was even more worrying. She had never given him reason to believe that they had anything other than friendship. She was fond of him, yes, owed him a great deal, but anything more, no—and to imply otherwise was distressing.

Emotionally drained after her husband's death, shocked and bewildered to discover that she was also pregnant, without a family to rely on, with no close friends nearby because they had only moved to the area shortly before Andrew's death, it had been Daniel, a childhood friend of her husband, who had supported her during and after the funeral.

She had allowed him to stay in the annexe adjoining her house, used his shoulder to lean on. When he'd heard her crying in the night, he'd come in, made tea, offered sympathy. It had been Daniel who had paced the hospital corridor when she'd had Riffy, like any proud father, but he wasn't the father, he was a friend, *only* a friend—but by then a lot of the damage had been done.

And when she'd begun to feel again, see more clearly, she'd seen the danger too late. A kind girl, she had not known how to be brutal. And then had come the car crash, and now Daniel was capitalising on that.

'I have to make a phone call.'

Turning, she stared blankly at Joshua. 'What?'

'I said, I have to make a phone call.'

'Oh, right,' she said lamely.

'I'll meet you outside.'

Not knowing what response was required, if any, she stood stupidly whilst he continued to stare at her, allowed his gaze to travel over her exquisite features, linger on her lips in a sensual appraisal that melted her insides. Then his eyes returned to hers and she found it hard to look away, began to feel isolated, out of her depth. Nervous.

His eyes were so brown, such a dark brown, the lashes thick, and his mouth was—finely drawn, beautiful, stern. It was a mouth that had touched hers, caressed hers...

With a little jerk, she blinked, stared at him warily, then quickly looked away. 'I have to get Riffy,' she mumbled distractedly.

'Yes. Rent me the cottage.'

'What?' Shocked, almost uncomprehending, she repeated numbly, 'What?'

'I want to be near you. Rent me the cottage.'

CHAPTER TWO

'No!' BROGAN denied hoarsely.

'You need to clear it with Daniel?'

'Of course I don't!'

'Then why? You said you were intending to rent it out.'

'*One* day! Not now, not yet. Joshua, you *know* what sort of state it's in!'

'I don't mind roughing it.'

'That wouldn't be roughing it,' she protested frantically. 'That would be—primitive!'

He smiled, trailed one long finger down her cheek. 'Why so frightened? Afraid Daniel might object?'

'I'm not frightened,' she denied, 'and it has nothing to do with Daniel!'

'Sure?'

'Of course I'm sure! Joshua, be sensible; you can't rent the cottage!'

'But I want to be near you,' he said softly. 'Want to be able to—'

'Don't,' she groaned. 'You mustn't.'

'Why?'

'Because... because...'

'There is something between you and Daniel?'

'No! And don't keep bringing Daniel into the conversation. It has nothing to do with him. The

cottage isn't fit for human habitation—you know
it isn't! It hasn't been lived in for years!'

'I don't mind.'

'Of course you do!' Despite non-designer jeans,
an unnamed shirt, there was an air of elegance
about him, a hint of excellence, and he looked as
though he'd mind a dropped hair, let alone months
of accumulated grime. 'Oh, Joshua, why?' she
wailed.

'You know why. You—excite me.'

Hot, disturbed, with an awful sliding feeling in
her tummy, she argued feebly, 'Can't you stay in
the village?'

'No,' he said softly. 'It's too far away. Go and
collect your daughter. I'll meet you outside.'

Her eyes following his tall figure as he strode to
the corner and picked up his battered haversack
which he had once told her contained all his worldly
possessions, she bit her lip, hard. Oh, Brogan, you
really must learn to have more will-power, she castigated herself weakly. Daniel pushes you around,
and now you're allowing Joshua to push you
around, and you don't know what he *wants*—not
really. Perhaps he couldn't *afford* to stay in the
village. Perhaps it was a plot to *rob* her. Hah! of
what? she wondered. She didn't *have* anything.

'Brogan!'

Whirling round, she stared somewhat blankly at
Daniel, then sighed, reached for her sleeping
daughter. 'Ready?'

'*I* am, yes. What did *he* want?'

'To rent the cottage,' she said without thinking.

'What?'

'Oh, don't you start,' she retorted tiredly. 'He wants to rent the cottage.'

'Has he *seen* it?'

'Yes, of course.'

'And he still wants to rent it?'

'Yes!'

'Why?' he demanded suspiciously. 'Why would a man who looks as though he's just come from the Ritz, stepped off his yacht—'

'Don't be absurd; he doesn't have a yacht.'

'Well, thank goodness for that. And there was me thinking he might sneer at the sight of a tumbledown cottage with no thatch on the roof! Brogan, be sensible; he can't stay in the cottage.'

'Well, he is. And he doesn't in the least look as though he could afford to stay in the Ritz. You only have to look at him once to see that.'

'I have, and he does. I've met people like him before. People who go slumming because they're bored.'

'Oh, don't be daft. And we have to go,' she added irritably. 'He'll be waiting.'

'Then let him wait. How long have you known him?'

'Long enough, and don't *interrogate* me! He needs to be in the area; some people are rebuilding a Norman keep or something. He's an historical architect. Or is it conservation?' She frowned.

'I don't care if he owns the National Trust! He can't stay in the cottage!'

'It's all arranged.'

'Then unarrange it!'

'No.' Scooping up her bag, she looped it over her shoulder. Cutting short any further discussion or argument, shifting her sleeping daughter into a more comfortable position, she awkwardly hefted his design case and walked out.

This had to stop. This really did have to stop. He was taking over her life! It was absolutely nothing to do with Daniel if she wanted to rent out the cottage. Coming to an abrupt halt, she stared despairingly at nothing. Rent him the cottage? How had she come round to that conclusion? She didn't *want* to rent him the cottage!

'Brogan!'

With an irritable twitch, she moved on. Why do you have to be so *perverse*, Brogan? she asked herself. Just because Daniel pooh-poohed it, it doesn't mean you have to take the opposite tack! Feeling steamrollered, she shoved open the heavy outer door.

Joshua was waiting. Leaning against his battered car, he smiled at Brogan, nodded to Daniel and explained languidly, 'Change of plan. I'll be down in a few days.' His eyes said things that his voice didn't and she flushed, wished he didn't have the power to make her feel like this. Wished... With a long sigh, she watched him get into his car and drive away.

'I'll go and get the car,' she said quietly. She laid Riffy in Daniel's arms and walked round to the next street to collect her old Renault. Daniel blamed her for the accident, trod all over her sensibilities, but it didn't stop him wanting her to drive him around, did it? Odd, that.

When they were loaded up, the wheelchair and the collection safely stowed, she climbed thankfully behind the wheel. Despite the accident, she wasn't nervous about driving—and Daniel didn't seem nervous about being her passenger, which was even odder.

He didn't speak much on the long drive up to Suffolk, for which she was grateful; he just stared from the window, a preoccupied frown on his face. He was the same age as she, but seemed younger, certainly acted younger sometimes—like a thwarted child. And how would you act, Brogan, if you had to spend your life in a wheelchair? she asked herself. As bitter as Daniel sometimes seemed, probably. But she couldn't change it, couldn't roll back time; all she could do was be there for him, help where she could.

The sound of the wheels on the tarmac was soporific and she forced herself to remain alert, pay attention, and at the back of her mind was the thought of Joshua. Joshua, who was coming to stay in the cottage. Joshua, whom Daniel seemed to think was slumming. Absurd, she decided dismissively. What would be the point? There were much more interesting places to slum than her old cottage.

Chelmsford, Braintree, Sudbury, and nearly home. She took the last turning towards Lavenham, swung into the lane and in through the gate-posts. With a long sigh, tired and dispirited, she switched off the engine and lights.

She could just make out the outline of the cottage from where she was parked, and the moonlight wasn't kind. It didn't soften the edges, clothe it in romance; it just highlighted its deplorable state of repair.

And wasn't one guest enough for her—non-paying at that? Now, because of her arbitrary behaviour, she was about to get another, who, she suspected, only wanted to pay her in kind. Fighting to squash the churning feeling that thoughts of Joshua always produced, she pushed open her door.

'I can't even offer to carry your bag,' Daniel commented bitterly.

'I don't need you to carry it, and you look as tired as I feel. It wasn't only a long day for Riffy.'

'Poryphia,' he corrected her.

'Yes,' she agreed. Why argue?

She unfolded the wheelchair, helped Daniel into it, picked up the case containing his collection and carried it to the door of the annexe. Returning for her daughter, she unclipped her, hefted her into her arms and locked the car. Not that anyone was likely to steal it. Car thieves were extraordinarily selective nowadays. As were joyriders. And they wouldn't get much joy riding in hers.

'Goodnight, Daniel,' she said quietly.

'Do you need any help with the baby?'

'No. Go and get some sleep.'

Quickly opening the front door, she slipped inside. Dropping her bag, she carried Riffy up to the nursery. Carefully changing her and popping her into her sleeping-suit, she laid her in her cot, loosely covered her with the quilt, and kissed her goodnight. Returning downstairs, she made herself a cup of tea and carried it up to her bedroom.

As she got ready for bed, she wondered, not for the first time, how to get herself out of a mess of her own making. She did Daniel's washing, ironing and shopping, because how could she have offered less when she'd been responsible for his being in a wheelchair? How could she have offered less than to let him continue to use the annexe when his own flat was on the third floor with no lift? And he'd been so incredibly kind when Andrew had died.

He could shower and dress himself, cook, make himself tea, but more often than not he came in to her, and now, because there was no time for anything else—to make new friends, meet new people—there *was* only Daniel. And that was wrong, restricting, making her into a person she was not meant to be. Making *him* into a person he was not meant to be.

She'd been gregarious, full of fun and hope, and now look at her. Married barely a year, widowed at twenty-six, a mother at twenty-seven, now twenty-eight, she seemed morally tied to a man who wanted to run her life for her, had convinced himself that he had the right to do so. And now, because she'd been afraid of what his reaction might be if she told him the truth about Joshua, she had lied, said he was a friend. And, of course, he wasn't. He was a—pursuer. And renting him the cottage was a really good way to put him off, wasn't it?

If Andrew could have seen the mess she was in, he'd have been horrified—no, he wouldn't. At least be honest, she told herself; don't turn Andrew into the saint he never was. He would have told her that it was her own fault. Which it probably was. Only, if she didn't rent Joshua the cottage, she might never see him again—and she wanted to. Despite her words to herself and to him, she did want to see him again. And that was probably very dumb.

Was he going to pay, though? She was getting through the insurance money at an alarming rate. The house was hers because they'd bought it outright; no building society would have given them a mortgage on it anyway. But there were still the bills, the day-to-day living expenses, and with a small baby it was very difficult to get any decorating done, to make it attractive at least inside, make it comfortable for paying guests.

And that brought her back to Joshua. Flirting briefly with the thought of what she could do with the money if he did pay her, she shook her head defeatedly. Money or no, he was another complication that she could have done without. Anyway, he'd only seen the cottage briefly, and when he saw it for *real*—well, he would probably flee in horror, as any sensible person would. And he certainly seemed sensible.

The next day, dressed in an old and faded cotton dress, hair dragged back unflatteringly, and with Riffy clambering enthusiastically round the furniture, Brogan cleaned the cottage, and ordered a new bed, because, really, even though she didn't want him there she could hardly expect him to sleep on the sagging monstrosity that was *in situ*, even if it *was* clean. She even managed to find someone who would deliver that day, and, with her ancient washing machine dealing, however reluctantly, with bedspread and curtains, she cleaned the windows and even managed to tidy the flower-bed that fronted the cottage.

Yet even with all her ministrations it didn't exactly shriek 'Welcome'! She didn't even know why she was *bothering*. She had more than enough to do without all this extra work, and by the time she'd ironed the curtains, rehung them, ironed the bedspread and put it ready to go on the new bed she felt exhausted.

She gave Riffy her lunch, lay her in her pram for a nap, and began on her own and the baby's washing. How very domestic, she thought with a tired smile. Who would have thought a few years ago that her life would change so dramatically? Her own little soft-furnishing business, newly married... Well, it was no good thinking about might-have-beens, and she wouldn't be without Riffy for the world.

Grabbing the polishing paraphernalia, she began on the hall, then the lounge, and lovingly polished the only piece of decent furniture she possessed—a round walnut dining table with six matching chairs. It had belonged to her mother—her mother who had also died, along with her father, years and years ago now. The Grim Reaper had certainly cut a giant swathe through her immediate family. And she had no brothers or sisters, only two elderly aunts who lived in Yorkshire. And Riffy. Adorable Riffy.

Catching a glimpse of her appalling appearance in a mirror, she pulled a face, and went to see if her daughter was awake—and found the kitchen flooded.

Oh, not today, please not today, she pleaded too late. Grabbing the nearest mopping-up equipment—a pile of freshly washed and dried towels—she flung them down to soak up the water, switched off the machine and hastened to ring the local repair man.

The bed arrived. The repair man didn't. Riffy woke, Daniel wanted to know why he hadn't been called to lunch, and the look she gave him sent him wheeling away in haste.

With Riffy playing in the garden in a makeshift play-pen, which wouldn't keep her confined for very long, judging by the way she was investigating how it lifted when she poked her fingers beneath it, Brogan managed to mop up the worst of the water, then gave a sigh of relief when someone knocked at the door. At last! Dropping the towel, she hurried to let him in.

'And about time too...' she began aggressively before actually registering who she was glaring at. 'Oh, sorry, I thought you were the repair man,' she mumbled. Flustered, mortifyingly aware of her dreadful appearance, she bit her lip and held the door wide for Joshua to enter. 'I look a mess—' she began, then broke off, furious with herself. She didn't need to *apologise*. 'You said a few days.'

Eyes steady, intent, that little smile pulling at his mouth, he queried softly, 'Did I?'

'Yes.'

'My plans changed.'

'Oh, well, you'd better come through. I've left the ba—' Hearing a wail, she broke off and ran.

'Oh, my God.' Sprinting down the garden, she grabbed Riffy from the top of the slide—the slide she had told Daniel to dismantle days ago when he had made it, the slide Riffy was too young for, the slide Brogan didn't *want*—and roared ominously, 'Daniel?'

And when Daniel had wheeled himself round the corner—reluctantly, judging by the expression on his face—she castigated him wrathfully, 'I told you to dismantle it! She could have been *killed*! I *told* you she was too young. I do wish you'd *listen*! And fancy leaving her unattended.'

'*I* didn't leave her unattended,' he said self-righteously. 'And I told you I couldn't look after her today. I'm *busy*.'

'I didn't ask you to look after her! And how did she get out of her play-pen?' she demanded rather unfairly. 'Oh, go back to your sewing!'

'Designing,' he corrected her. With a last glare, he wheeled himself away, and if a person in a wheelchair could be said to flounce then Daniel certainly managed it.

Setting her daughter on the grass, Brogan grabbed the offending slide and dragged it to the shed. Opening the door, she shoved it inside, then slammed the door shut. Making sure the catch was down, she turned and found herself face to face with Joshua. Joshua, who made her feel inadequate.

'He keeps *making* her things,' she declared in lame explanation. 'Sorry,' she muttered even more ungraciously. 'It's been one of those days.' And a man in a blue overall was hovering by her back door, she saw. 'About time!' she exclaimed. 'Excuse me,' she muttered to Joshua. 'Won't be a minute. Watch Riffy, will you?'

Hurrying in, she pointed to the washing machine, gave the man a vague smile, and hurried back. Riffy was making a spirited attempt to climb his leg, which Joshua was ignoring. Picking her daughter up, she sighed defeatedly. 'I'll show you the cottage. I haven't had time to...

'Oh, now what?' she exclaimed tiredly as the repair man wandered out in the obvious expectation of having a word. 'No, no, don't tell me,' she derided him sarcastically. 'You don't have the right parts. What is it with you people? I *said* it was the door seal. I specifically *said* that! And if you're about to tell me you can't fix it today, please don't—I need it. And I'm not paying *two* call-out charges!'

'I just wanted to know if you'd had any trouble with it before today,' he murmured meekly, 'because it isn't actually the seal.'

'Oh. No. It just—flooded.'

'Right you are.'

When he'd gone back inside, she returned her attention to Joshua, who was watching her, and she flushed. 'All right, all right,' she muttered defensively, 'you don't have to say it. I *know* I was rude, but...'

'I make you nervous,' he completed for her.

'Yes. No. I don't understand why you're here!' she blurted out. 'You don't seem at all the sort of man who would be interested in a widow with a baby.'

'Don't I?' he queried lazily. 'What sort of man *do* I seem?'

'I don't *know*!'

Swinging away from a regard that was uncomfortable, she stared at the cottage. Well, it *was* a cottage, she thought defiantly. Of sorts. A bit sad-looking, maybe—a bit dilapidated, a bit small, but then, it was old. He should feel right at home, shouldn't he, seeing as he was an historical architect?

Glancing at him sideways to gauge his reaction, she was unable to read anything from a face that was totally expressionless. About to apologise, hastily explain, she bit her lip, remembered what Daniel had said, forced herself to remain quiet. And he didn't have to take it, did he? He could *refuse*.

He examined the cottage for what felt like an eternity, then looked at her, his eyes unfathomable.

'It's better inside,' she muttered. 'Clean and—well, comfortable. The bed's new,' she added, and was angry with herself for trying to defend something that was, quite frankly, indefensible. 'It's not locked.'

'Nothing to steal?'

Not deigning to answer, deciding it wasn't *worth* answering, she pointed to the track that meandered rather than ran round the side of the house to the back of the cottage. 'It has its own access. You can park your car at the back.'

'A bonus.'

'Stop *laughing* at me! You laugh at me *inside*, where it doesn't *show*, and if you aren't laughing then you're being sarcastic! You don't *have* to stay here. It's not compulsory!'

His mouth twitched.

'And beggars can't be choosers!'

He looked at her, gave her a smile that wasn't any sort of smile at all. 'You or me?' he drawled.

Face set, trying frantically to think of a cutting answer and failing, she looked away.

'Where's Daniel?'

'Hiding,' she said shortly before she could get a grip on her unruly tongue. 'He lives in the annexe.'

The eyebrow went up. He turned to look at the house, the annexe, then back to the cottage.

'I *told* you it was falling down!' she blurted out defensively.

'So you did.'

'Yes. Well, I expect you'll want to find somewhere else. Go back where you were...'

'I don't like hotels. A hundred a week?'

'A hundred?' she queried in astonishment. 'You intend to *pay* me?'

'Of course. Have to keep it above board, don't we?'

Did they?

'Have we stood here long enough?' he asked in amusement.

'What?'

'I assumed we were trying to give the impression of a business transaction. For Daniel's benefit.'

'Well, we weren't! And why do you keep bringing Daniel into every conversation?' she demanded aggrievedly. 'It isn't anything to *do* with him! And you can't really want to stay here, Joshua,' she added weakly. 'I mean, *look* at it!'

'I am,' he said with a rueful smile. 'You'd rather I stayed in the house?'

'No!'

His smile widened. Removing his car keys from his pocket, quickly holding them out of Riffy's reach when she lunged for them, he said softly, 'I'll get the car.'

Watching him walk away, Brogan gave a dispirited sigh. Perhaps he was grateful to be near his work, wherever that was. Then she gave a lame smile. Joshua Baynard and grateful would *never* be on the same mailing list—and she wasn't the stuff of which landladies were made.

But to actually *pay* her... Because he thought her a charity case? Although, a charity case was what she undoubtedly looked like, she thought despairingly. She hadn't even had time to wash her hair—hardly a very good impression to give. Not that she *wanted* to impress him, she assured herself. Yet even with her hair unwashed she was still, even though she didn't realise it, a very beautiful young woman—with large, somewhat wistful, grey eyes, brown curly hair, high cheekbones, and a mouth she thought too wide.

Daniel wheeled himself out from the annexe, and she braced herself for yet another argument.

'Was that Joshua?' he demanded. 'Why didn't you tell me he was coming today?'

'I didn't know he was coming today.'

'Well, what did he say?'

'Nothing.'

'He must have said *something*!'

'Well, he didn't. I wonder if I'm supposed to feed him?' she murmured worriedly.

'Feed him?' he echoed. 'Why would you want to feed him?'

'I don't *want* to!' she denied in exasperation. 'I was just wondering if I was *supposed* to.'

'He's taking it?'

'Mmm. A hundred a week.'

'A hundred? Is he mad?'

'Probably.'

'Then make sure you stay away from him!'

'Oh, Daniel...'

'I mean it, Brogan. A young woman on her own—'

'I'm not *on* my own.'

'To all intents and purposes,' he said bitterly. '*I* can't defend you, can I?'

'I don't need you to defend me, and this argument is singularly pointless. Go and finish your designing. I have things to do.' Like putting clean sheets and towels in the cottage... Oh, hell. She'd *known* there was something else she had to do.

Walking inside, she stared at the washing-machine components spread across the floor, at one of her best towels still lying where she'd left it after using it to mop up the water, and wondered whether to scream now or later.

The repair man looked up, smiled, and, as though her appearance required something other than squatting on the floor, he wiped his hands, stood, smiled at the baby, and eyed the kettle. Hopefully.

Giving in, she asked fatalistically, 'Tea?'

'Thought you'd never ask. Hot today.'

'Yes.' It was more than hot—it was humid, sticky, and she wanted the day to be over. Only half listening as he began a dissertation on flimsy workmanship, equipment that didn't last and how rubber perished when it shouldn't, she sat Riffy on the floor, gave her a wooden spoon to play with and made the tea.

'Got insurance, have you, love?'

Staring at him, her heart sank. 'No, and that sounded like an expensive question.'

He sucked his teeth. 'We-ell, I can't get round the cost of the spare parts, but . . .' With a wink which Brogan wasn't sure she shouldn't be alarmed about, he commented, 'Nice baby.'

'Yes,' she agreed inadequately. 'Well, I'll leave you to get on.' With a vague smile, she went to collect clean sheets and towels, and with Riffy under one arm, linen under the other she walked down to the cottage. Not really thinking, her mind busy juggling finances, praying that the repairs wouldn't come to more than she had, she lightly tapped and walked in on her newly acquired guest—who was wearing a towel. *Only* a towel. And a very small one at that. Fortunately, he was wearing it round his hips.

'Oh. Sorry.' Flustered, looking everywhere but at a naked expanse of chest and equally naked long legs, she mumbled, 'Clean towels and sheets.'

'Thank you,' he murmured drily. 'A little earlier might have been helpful.'

'Yes. Sorry,' she repeated. 'I forgot.' Dumping them on the nearest chair, she turned to hurry away.

His voice stopped her. It was a voice that she was coming to dislike intensely.

'The water was cold.'

Oh, God. Keeping her back to him, she explained, 'There's an immersion heater.'

'So I discovered. What I did not discover was the switch.'

'Oh. I would have done it, but—'

'You didn't know I was coming today,' he completed for her. 'Yes, you said.'

Her face still averted, her mouth pursed, she walked into the bathroom—a bathroom barely bigger than a shower stall—awkwardly opened the airing cupboard, groped around at the back, located the switch and flicked it on just as Riffy grabbed the slat above her that doubled as a shelf and pulled it off.

'Ow!' Rubbing her sore head, she closed her eyes in defeat. She didn't want to be here. She didn't want *him* in her life, she didn't want *Daniel* in her life, or a washing-machine repair man, and, above all, she didn't want to look as stupid as she was beginning to look in front of a man who—unnerved her.

She wasn't stupid, she was highly intelligent, but she'd had a day like no other. The kitchen floor still hadn't been mopped, and with her luck the repair man would slip and break his leg. She had a guest she didn't want—a guest who stood behind her, naked but for a towel, a guest who gave her thoughts she shouldn't have, didn't want to have, need to have—and grizzling felt imminent. No, grizzling felt entirely desirable.

Picking up the shelf, she replaced it, closed the cupboard door, and aware, so very aware, that Joshua Baynard was standing too close, that if she turned... A long finger touched her neck and she jumped. That same long finger eased the neck of her dress aside, and a warm mouth pressed the softest of kisses to her shoulder.

'You've stopped breathing,' he murmured on a laugh.

Oh, God, and Riffy—wretched Riffy—lunged over her other shoulder and grabbed his hair.

'Dad, Dad, *Dad*,' she shrieked gleefully, and Joshua lifted her across, held her easily in one arm, turned Brogan, drew her close, looked into her eyes, and kissed her. Not swiftly, not chastely, but with a thorough exploration that left her feeling mindless—and his long fingers were doing the most incredible things to the back of her neck.

His mouth left hers slowly, reluctantly, and amusement shone in his eyes. 'She's wet.'

'What?'

'Your daughter.' His soft, seductive eyes still holding hers, he repeated, 'She's wet.'

'Oh, right, yes. I mean—it's water, from the washing machine, not...' With a ragged sigh, she took her daughter back, shook her head defeatedly and walked out. 'Monkey,' she muttered to her unrepentant daughter, eyes still blank, dazed. 'And that is not Daddy.'

Daddy hadn't looked in the least like Joshua. But then Riffy had never seen her daddy, only a photograph of him. Riffy never would see her daddy and so couldn't be blamed, Brogan supposed, for thinking that any man who came within her orbit might be him. But what did he want? What, ultimately, did he want?

Walking into the kitchen—a tidied kitchen—she tried to pull herself together. 'All finished?' she asked the repair man hopefully. 'How much do I owe you?'

He smiled, ruffled the baby's sparse fair hair. 'Fifty should do it. I'll lose the rest.'

'Oh...' Feeling almost overwhelmed at such kindness, she managed a smile. 'What was it? And don't I have to pay a call-out fee?'

'Nah—don't charge 'em. Couldn't compete with the big firms otherwise.'

'Oh, well, thank you,' she said with a warm smile. Perhaps wearing an old dress hadn't been a mistake after all. Finding her bag, taking out her cheque-book, she registered his expression and hesitated. 'No cheque?'

He looked a bit embarrassed. 'Rather have cash if you've got it. Only the missus asked me to get some shopping on the way back...'

And he didn't have any more money than she did. Oh, boy. This place was beginning to feel like a refugee station. 'Hang on a minute.' Hurrying round to the annexe, she burst in. 'Daniel, have you got any cash on you?'

Looking up from his sketch-pad, his face somewhat blank, he stared at her as though he'd never seen her before. 'Hmm?'

'Have you got any cash?'

He shook his head. 'Fiver.'

'No, that's no good. Oh, knickers!'

'What do you want it for?'

'The repair man.'

'Sorry, can't help,' he said indifferently. 'Why don't you ask your other quest?'

'Don't sneer. And I can't ask him.'

'Why not?'

'Because I can't.'

'Why?' Joshua asked from behind her.

Swinging round, she stared at him helplessly. 'Because it's not...'

'Ethical?'

'Yes. No. Oh, I need fifty pounds,' she muttered in embarrassment.

'Why don't you give her an advance on the rent?' Daniel put in nastily. 'You are paying rent, I believe?'

'Mmm.' Glancing from one to the other, that small, *irritating* smile playing about his mouth, he removed his wallet from his back pocket and handed over five ten-pound notes. 'You can give me the receipt later.'

'Receipt? Oh, yes—thank you.' Grabbing the money, she fled. And at least he'd been dressed. Close-fitting grey trousers, short-sleeved blue shirt. Bare feet. Small scar on his collar-bone.

Bursting back into the kitchen, unconscious of how comprehensive her glance at Joshua must have been, she handed the money over and smiled. 'Sorry it took so long—had to borrow.'

'You won't be short yourself?' the repair man asked worriedly.

'No, no, I'll go to the bank.' And would be told that she'd exceeded this month's allowance. And whose bright idea had it been for the bank to manage her affairs?

Seeing him out, thanking him once again, she closed the door, then leaned back against it with a sigh. All she wanted to do was sit down, put her feet up, but she had Riffy to feed and a kitchen floor to mop—and the phone to answer. It was for Daniel. Well, it would be, wouldn't it? She just *wished* he would answer his own line. He'd had it put in, for goodness' sake!

When she'd fetched him, she set about feeding her daughter. Sitting Riffy in her high chair to keep her out of mischief whilst she cooked mince and potatoes, Brogan sang nursery rhymes to her and giggled at the extraordinary faces that her daughter pulled because she had discovered that they made people laugh. Even at barely a year, she had learned the art of showing off.

'Round and round the garden, like a teddy bear... There's a clever girl. One step, two step—'

'That was the photographer,' Daniel announced abruptly. 'He... Good God, Brogan, what on earth are you cooking her?'

'Mince.'

'It looks revolting.'

'She likes it. What did the photographer want?'

'To do the shoot next Sunday. I've rung up Amanda—'

'Amanda?'

'One of the waitresses at the Swan.'

'Oh, right.'

'And she's asking some friends to help out, model the outfits. So if you'll do the black rubber again...'

'Oh, no. Oh, no, Daniel, I am not getting into that straight-jacket again. It's much too hot.'

'It won't be; we're doing it at seven in the morning.'

'I can't get there at *seven*,' she protested. Turning out the heat, giving the meal a last stir, she dished it up into Riffy's bowl and set it aside to cool whilst she boiled her milk.

'You promised.'

'I did *not* promise.'

'Oh, great,' he said bitterly. 'Fine portfolio I'll have with only four outfits in it!'

'Don't sulk. Why can't one of the other girls wear it?'

'Because they'll be either too short or too plump!'

'You don't know that.'

'Yes, I do!'

'What comes next?' a cool, derisive voice asked from behind them. 'My dad's a policeman?'

The both swung round, and Daniel demanded rudely, 'What do you want?'

'A key.'

'What for? No one's going to burgle the damned place.'

'You're omniscient?' Joshua asked admiringly.

Daniel flushed, gave Brogan an angry look and wheeled himself out.

'That was uncalled for,' she said crossly. 'And I'm not sure there is a key, but any that came with the house are in that drawer. You're welcome to look. If there isn't one, please feel free to have the lock changed,' she invited him stiffly. 'At my expense, of course.'

'Of course.'

'Oh, shut up.'

Opening the drawer indicated, he rummaged through the rubbish shoved in there—old paper bags, pegs, washers, and even, for goodness' sake, a bicycle pump. All she needed really was the bicycle to go with it. What she would have *liked* was a poisoned dart. Pulling up a stool, she perched in front of her daughter and began to feed her. Messily. Her daughter was *not* a dainty eater.

'I forgot to stock up your fridge,' she confessed haughtily. 'Do you need milk or something? Or I could make you a cup of tea... Oh, Riffy, don't do that,' she pleaded weakly when her daughter pushed the food out with her tongue. 'Eat it nicely, there's a good girl.' Aware of silence behind her, she turned and found Joshua watching the performance with an amused smile. He was holding a selection of keys.

'I'll try these if I may.'

She nodded, slumped tiredly when he walked out. Oh, boy. He made her feel like a limp cabbage. Green and useless and unattractive. And what *did* he need keys for? Afraid someone might snoop?

'I used to be smart, Riffy,' she murmured wistfully. 'Bright and bubbly with lots and lots of things to say. I could talk to people like Joshua Baynard with no trouble at all. I *worked* for people like Joshua Baynard, and I don't remember that I ever felt inadequate— Don't do that, you wretch, and don't beam with your mouth full.' With a little grunt of laughter, she gave Riffy the last spoonful, wiped her sticky face and hands, and gave her her milk to hold. 'And don't dob it. Drink it.'

'I need someone to talk to,' she continued as she began to assemble a rather doubtful-looking salad. 'Someone who answers back—not arguing, like Daniel, but talking, exchanging ideas. And much as I love you, Riffy, you aren't the greatest conversationalist in the world.'

Sucking enthusiastically on her bottle, her daughter watched her, eyes round and interested.

Putting some eggs on to boil to make the salad look more appetising, Brogan briefly wondered whether she was supposed to offer Joshua some, then denied the thought. Let him eat out; she wasn't going to have that disparaging face sneer at her culinary efforts.

He sneered anyway, or she thought he did, when he returned with the keys. Then she felt a stab of guilt. Perhaps he couldn't afford to eat out. Perhaps she'd just appropriated his last fifty pounds. Perhaps the sneer had been caused by *hunger*. There had to be a *reason* for this nightmare.

'Find anything?'

'Mmm.'

She nodded, searched his face, tried to find *something* in his non-expression apart from hateful amusement. 'Would you like something to eat? It's only salad I'm afrai—' She broke off, her mouth tightening, when he glanced rather disparagingly at the meal and shuddered—definitely shuddered.

Returning the rest of the keys to the drawer, he carefully closed it, and, his hands still resting on the old wood, he asked, 'Why does he live in the annexe?'

'What?'

'Daniel. Why does he live in the annexe?'

'Because I don't want him living here. Besides, the doctors said it was best for him to have some independence.'

'Ah.'

'*If* it's any business of yours,' she added pointedly.

The smile appeared and she looked quickly away, hastily tried to field the bottle which Riffy threw and missed. Joshua, didn't. Well, he wouldn't, would he? Probably played cricket or something. Probably played for *England*!

A laugh in his voice, he said, 'I'm not *trying* to make you feel inadequate.'

'Well, you're succeeding.' Snatching the bottle from him, she returned it to her daughter. 'No,' she said firmly. 'Naughty.' Riffy beamed, banged her bottle on the tray. 'Dad, Dad, *Dad*,' she shrieked, and gave Joshua one of her best facial expressions. Joshua looked unimpressed.

Turning to Brogan, he asked softly, 'Receipt?'

'*Receipt*? You really want one?'

'Mmm.'

'What do you think I'm going to do? Run off without paying you back? I'll give it to you tomorrow. I don't have a receipt book. I wasn't expecting to get paid!'

'What were you expecting, Brogan?' he asked even more softly.

'Nothing!'

He gave a little grunt that might have been laughter, advanced, kissed her nose. 'You're a very strange lady.'

'I'm a very *tired* lady,' she corrected him crossly.

He smiled, waggled his fingers at Riffy and walked out.

'Bastard,' she muttered, too softly for Riffy to hear. 'Supercilious, unfeeling bastard.' Did he think she was in the *habit* of borrowing money?

'And if you ever,' she told Daniel a few minutes later when he wheeled himself in, 'arbitrarily stick your oar into things not your concern you can leave. The hair-shirt is wearing thin, Daniel. Very thin! Eat your salad.'

He ate his salad.

'Sunday?' he asked quietly as he was about to leave. 'Please? Just once more?'

About to refuse, knowing she couldn't, hurt by the plea in his eyes—a plea she had put there—she gave a reluctant nod. 'But that's the last time I wear it,' she warned. 'Sunday, and then no more.'

'OK. Thanks, Brogan.' Smiling at Riffy, he wheeled himself out.

I want my life back, she thought. Dear God, but I want my life back. And never had a day seemed so long.

She got Riffy settled down by nine, and herself into bed by ten with the biggest sigh of relief imaginable—the biggest sigh of *thanks*. Perhaps there would be no need to see much of Joshua. If he was working all day... And oh, for an uninterrupted night's sleep, she prayed.

The prayer went unanswered.

CHAPTER THREE

THE explosive crack snapped Brogan awake in shock and panic. Red after-images distorted her vision. She held her breath until her mind interpreted the sound, then released it slowly, and only then did her heart stagger back to normal, until the next crack of thunder only seconds later. Riffy screamed and Brogan stumbled from the bed and along the landing to the nursery.

Picking her up, she soothed her, flinched when jagged forks of lightning split the night sky apart, hugged her daughter closer. They'd forecast storms, but this was Armageddon! The noise was incredible!

Fascinated despite herself, she watched the next spear of light, gave a funny little laugh as it stabbed down from the heavens and looked as though it hit the cottage, and then her laugh died, because it *had* hit the cottage. Oh, God. That was Joshua's bedroom! For a moment—long seconds that felt like eternity—she was incapable of constructive thought, was merely disbelieving. Supposing...

Staring down at her daughter, seeing that, unbelievably, she had gone back to sleep, Brogan gently returned her to her cot and ran. Barefoot, wearing only a skimpy nightie, she flung herself across the grass, into the cottage, into his bedroom, and halted. Breathing heavily, she stared at the ragged hole in the wall, the bricks and rubble that littered the bed, forced her shocked mind to contemplate death, injury...

'Bit of a mess,' a laconic voice murmured from behind her.

Swinging round, she stared at Joshua. An all-right Joshua belting himself into a robe.

'I saw... I thought...'

'And the speedy reaction is much appreciated,' he said somewhat drily. 'What were you intending to do? Dig me out single-handed?'

'Don't sneer,' she retorted breathlessly. 'You think I couldn't?'

He paused, then said quietly, 'No.'

Swinging back to the wall, she stared at it. And when it rained, as it would... 'You can't stay here.'

'No.'

'You'd better come back to the house.'

'An overwhelming offer.'

'Stop it!' she said fiercely. 'I expected to find...'

He sighed. 'Yes. I'm sorry. It was something of a shock to me too.'

'You weren't hurt?'

He shook his head, watched her.

'I can make you up a bed on the sofa, or we could carry the bed across...' And now that the initial drama was over her mind felt incapable of constructive thought. She was aware of her skimpy nightie, his short robe—not much on either of them to cover nakedness—and suddenly there was electricity inside as well as outside. The distance between them was not great; the size of the cottage did not allow for huge distances between people and she was only an arm's reach away—a distance he took full advantage of.

'Is this for my benefit?' he asked softly as he touched one long finger to the strap of her nightdress.

'No,' she denied thickly. 'When I saw the lightning strike, I just ran. I thought you were dead.'

'And would you have minded?'

'Of course I would have minded!'

'Good.'

'Joshua, I—' she began urgently when he pulled her towards him, against him, held her loosely within the circle of his arms, breast to breast, thigh to thigh.

'Shh.' Bending his head, he captured her mouth, slid his hands up her back, let them rest briefly on her shoulder blades, moved one back to her waist, the other up to her neck, twisted it in her hair. 'I could love you here...'

'Ah, no,' she breathed against his mouth. 'No.' But her body had ideas of its own, melted against him, and her arms were somehow round his neck, her breasts against his chest, between his open robe, and he pressed one hard thigh between her legs, exciting her. It had been such a long time since she'd been loved, held like this, kissed like this—and it had *never* been like this, she thought hazily. Never, ever, ever...

His mouth moving on hers was tempting, tantalising, tormenting, his fingers pressing, teasing, and when his mouth moved to her neck she stared over his shoulder, eyes wide, dazed, yearning.

'I can't leave Riffy too long,' she whispered raggedly.

'No.'

'I could put her in with me...'

'Put me in with you,' he argued seductively, and
she groaned, shook her head weakly.

'No.' Trying to be sensible, she forced a small
amount of space between them, stared into his face.
'I can't think when you touch me like this,' she
objected thickly.

'I wasn't intending you to,' he murmured as he
continued to touch her, intimately—a shivering delight she kept trying to deny.

'And we can't leave the bed here,' she continued
desperately, hoarsely. 'When it rains...'

'Mmm,' he agreed absently as he continued his
exploration. Eyes so very dark, intent on hers, he
trailed his fingers across her shoulder, dislodged a
strap, continued down, and warmth flooded her
stomach, tightened her thighs.

'It will get wet,' she said raggedly. 'And there's
no room to put it in the tiny lounge; the cottage is
too sma— Oh, Joshua don't do that,' she groaned
weakly as warm fingers cupped the breast he had
exposed as his head dipped to savour it.

With a sharp intake of breath, she clutched him
tight, shuddered, fought not to give in to sensations that she had not felt for so long—sensations
she yearned to revel in. Surely there should be
shame in such delight, in allowing intimacies with
a virtual stranger?

'You don't like it?'

'No—yes. Oh, please don't; this could *destroy* me.'

He broke off, raised his head. 'Destroy?' he queried softly. 'An odd word to choose.'

'Choose?' she cried. 'Choose? It is not *choice*! I barely know you!'

'No,' he agreed—a soft little puff of sound, almost a sigh.

'And I don't *want* this!'

'Don't you?'

'No!'

'Why?'

'Because my life is complicated enough!' she cried.

Staring into her troubled face, he gave a slight nod and gently replaced the strap. 'And when you do know me? When your life is less complicated?' he asked softly.

'I don't know. I don't understand what's *happening*. You make me feel . . .'

'Yes,' he agreed. 'You make me feel too.'

Stepping back, she eyed him warily, saw his slight amusement—no, was *aware* of his amusement—she couldn't actually see his expression in the dim light—and felt a fool, naïve. And they couldn't stand here staring at each other for the rest of the night. She needed to get back in case Riffy woke.

Taking a deep breath, she turned to stare at the bed. 'Right,' she began briskly, then hastily cleared her throat because she sounded husky, breathless. 'We can carry the bed across, worry about everything else later.' Grabbing the coverlet, she stripped it off, shook out the debris, bundled up the rest of the bedding and walked out. Hurrying across the garden, flinching every time the lightning flashed, she dumped it in the kitchen, forced herself not to think or feel, and hurried back to help with the bed.

'Grab hold,' she instructed him, and fortunately didn't see his expression of amusement at her high-handed behaviour.

'It would be better to take the mattress first,' he said with quiet logic. 'Otherwise...'

Nodding, impatient now to get it over with, be on her own, try to *think*, she grabbed one end of the unwieldy mattress and struggled out behind him.

'Upstairs,' she instructed him once they were in the house.

'Can we put the light on?' he asked drily.

Mouth tight, furious with herself for her stupidity, embarrassed, aware that her nightdress was *short*, she struggled to balance the mattress one-handed, and reached out to snap on the switch before they made their way up the stairs.

'Leave it here on the landing,' she whispered so as not to wake her daughter, then changed her mind. 'No, if we take the cot out first, carrying it into my room, that will be best.' Nodding to herself, she carefully eased open Riffy's door, waited until Joshua had joined her, indicated for him to lift one end of the cot, then lifted the other.

Shuffling, they carried it along to her room and set it down by the wall furthest from the window. Riffy slept on. Tiptoeing out, Brogan carefully

eased her door shut and headed back down the
stairs, Joshua meekly following.

When they'd finally finished and the bed, newly
made up, was installed in Riffy's room, still
avoiding eye contact, she said quietly, awkwardly,
'Goodnight.'

'Goodnight. Do you have any polythene?' He
sounded hatefully amused.

'Polythene?' she queried blankly.

'To tack over the hole. When it rains...'

'Oh—yes. I think there's some in the shed.'

'And tools?'

'On the bench.' With some rather unformed idea
that she should offer to do it, she began, 'Shall
I...?'

'No. Go to bed.'

Nodding, she walked out and into her own room,
let out her breath on a long, shaky sigh, stared at
her hands, thought about her feet, and padded out
again and into the bathroom.

Life had been difficult—no, life had been a
bloody nuisance but bearable—until the advent of
Joshua. Don't think about it, she instructed herself
firmly. And, above all, don't let your mind linger
on the feel of him, the taste...

She dragged in a breath, held it, then released it
slowly. You don't *know* him, Brogan. You rushed
into marriage with Andrew... Don't be a fool.
Joshua doesn't want *marriage*. And neither do you.
Go to bed.

Climbing beneath the duvet, she glanced at the
clock. Two. With luck, she might get four hours'
sleep. If she could *get* to sleep. If she could forget

about being held in gentle arms, kissed as though tomorrow did not matter... With a groan, she buried her face in the pillow, tried to ignore the ache inside.

Barely an hour later, programmed to obey when she registered the small sounds—never mind *what* small sounds, because sounds in the night always meant Riffy—eyes not even open, she stumbled along to the nursery, groped for the cot—and remembered.

'Changed your mind?' Joshua asked softly.

She stared in his general direction, glanced at the baby alarm still connected, grunted, and padded back out. Riffy was still asleep.

Three o'clock. With luck, she might get *three* hours' sleep.

Riffy didn't know about luck, only about sore gums and a wet bottom.

Three-thirty. On automatic pilot, she laid Riffy back down, fell into bed, and from waking to sleeping—the line between them so ill defined as to be non-existent—reclaimed the arms of Morpheus.

Riffy slept till seven. Beautiful, adorable, smashing, wonderful Riffy slept till seven. It felt like five, but against all expectations she had managed another hour.

Staring at her daughter who was pulling faces at her through the bars of the cot, Brogan smiled—and thoughts of Joshua rushed in. Firmly dismissing them, she scrambled free of the covers. 'Come on, beaming pumpkin,' she laughed. 'Let's get another day started.' Lifting her daughter out,

she gave her a smacking kiss and carried her into
the bathroom. Running a few inches of water into
the bath, she sat Riffy at one end to play at
splashing whilst she had her shower—and Joshua
walked in.

She shrieked and didn't know where to hold the
sponge; Riffy shrieked and slapped the water. He
grinned, quietly apologised and retreated. He must
have *heard* them in here, she thought indignantly.
Perhaps he had voyeuristic tendencies...

Hurriedly finishing, she wrapped a towel round
her wet hair and put on a short silk robe to cover
her nakedness; then she washed and dried her
daughter, put on her nappy and carried her back
to the bedroom, snuggling the warm little body to
her. There was so much joy and pleasure in the feel
of a warm little body—so much joy and pleasure
in the feel of a warm, hard, *masculine* body... Shut
up, Brogan. A warm, *chubby* little body, she insisted to herself as she gave Riffy an extra hug.
'Mmm, I could eat you all *up*!'

Riffy gurgled, tried to strangle her. 'Mum, Mum,
Mum, Mum!'

'Mmm, Mum, Mum, Mum.' She grinned. 'I
think, Riffy Carpenter,' she said softly, 'that you
are something pretty special.' Lowering her to the
floor, she pulled back the curtains, stared out at
the new day. Grey cloud, no sun, still muggy.

Joshua was standing at the end of the cottage,
staring up at the wall, and her smile died. Did the
insurance cover lightning strikes? She wasn't sure
it did. And if it didn't... Don't trouble trouble till
trouble troubles you. Hah. And he'd been going to

pay her a hundred pounds to rent it, hadn't he? Very amusing, God. Thank you so much.

'Riffy, no!' Launching herself across the room, she managed to grab her daughter just as she was about to haul all the contents off the dressing table. 'No,' she repeated. 'Wretch. Come on; let's get you dressed. What you need is a strait-jacket, my girl. Think it's funny, do you? You're a *pickle*!' Tickling her until she was gurgling infectiously, she carried her into the nursery, laid her on the floor and began finding her clothes.

'No, no, no, no, no,' she laughed, and quickly grabbed her daughter before she could escape onto the landing. Dumping her onto the bed, she hastily found her dungarees and T-shirt, then began wrestling her into them.

'It is not a *game*, child! It's called getting *dressed*—'

'And it's probably all your own fault that she thinks it's a game in the first place,' Joshua pointed out, quite truthfully as it happened, from the open doorway. 'Go and get dressed.'

Opening her mouth to tell him to mind his own business or something, she watched the eyebrow ascend, glanced down at her robe that was hanging open at the front, and wrenched the two sides together.

'I'll watch her.' It wasn't an offer, it was a statement, and Riffy, fast to spot a moment's inattention, was off down the bed like an express train, and into Joshua's arms. He did not laugh at her, tickle her, kiss her, do any of the things people usually did when catching a baby, he merely looked at her, and Riffy—undiscerning Riffy—beamed at him and slapped his cheeks with a crow of delight.

He glanced at Brogan, amused *knowledge* on his face, waited, and with a cross tut she hurried out and into her bedroom to dress. Dragging on underwear, long shorts and a crop-sleeved top, she quickly dried her hair, dragged a brush through it, and, as though afraid that something dire might have happened to her daughter in her absence, hurried into the other bedroom, found them gone, and leapt down the stairs and into the lounge.

Skidding to a lame halt, she watched Joshua with her daughter. Crouched on the floor in front of her, he was building up her bricks, gently making her wait until he'd finished the small construction, and then allowing her to knock them down.

He glanced up at her unorthodox entrance, and she silently warned him against using his eyebrow. It was beginning to irritate her *very* much. Riffy didn't even look round, just screeched to gain Joshua's attention, and cleverly gave him a brick. At least, Brogan thought it was clever. Joshua looked as though it was no less than he expected.

'I'll start breakfast,' she said abruptly, and if he mentioned bursting in on her in the shower...

Going into the kitchen, she crashed things around until common sense restored her sense of proportion, then gave a shamefaced smile. Who's the child here, Brogan? she asked herself. You or Riffy? Perhaps he was playing tit for tat. She'd burst in on him, he'd burst in on her... Well, now they'd both seen the other naked—half-naked; he hadn't actually been naked... Will you shut up, Brogan?

'I've made the tea,' she said quietly a few minutes later. 'What will you have to eat? Toast? Cereal?'

'Toast will be fine.' Standing, he picked up Riffy, walked with her into the kitchen and put her in her high chair, then took a seat at the battered table that Brogan had started to strip ready for repolishing. She hadn't, yet, had time to finish it.

'Daniel doesn't join you for breakfast?' he asked quietly.

'Would you?' she asked with a laugh that rang false even to her own ears. 'Breakfast is usually somewhere around six-thirty.'

He didn't answer, but she could feel him watching her, feel amusement emanating from him, and that made her nervous, inclined to babble, which made her furious with herself, because she wasn't normally a babbler.

'We didn't discuss what arrangements you wanted for meals . . .'

'So we didn't,' he agreed blandly. 'But just breakfast will be fine. If I'm up first, or last, I'll get my own. If that's all right,' he tacked on.

'Oh, I meant just today. I assumed you would be going now that the cottage is uninhabitable . . . I mean, you can't stay here, in the house, can you?'

'Can't I?'

'No, and I'm sure you'll be able to find a room in Lavenham.'

'I don't like hotels,' he stated quietly.

'Oh, no. I forgot . . .'

'I would prefer to stay here. It will only be to sleep. I shall be out most of the day.'

'Oh.'

'Is that all right?'

No, she really didn't think it was, and how could one statement like 'It will only be to sleep' hold so many connotations? 'There's only one bathroom,' she said stupidly.

'I know. If there's a problem, I can use the one at the cottage. Can't I?'

'I suppose.' But she didn't *want* him here. The thought of him in the cottage had been bad enough. And he might at least *try* to see things from her point of view, not sound as though he thought that she was *stupid*. 'And what about washing?' she demanded as though *that* might be an insurmountable problem.

'I'm sure my landlady will allow me to use her washing machine. Won't she?'

'*You* use it? Do you know how?'

'I expect I can figure it out.'

'Yes.' Despairing, hating herself, she saw smoke begin to rise from the toaster and hastily lunged. 'Doesn't pop up,' she muttered. Rescuing the toast, she put it on a plate for him and handed it across.

'Are you always this indecisive?' he asked interestedly.

'Yes. No. Don't push your luck. And if you mention *routine*,' she added fiercely, 'I get violent!'

She wasn't used to people in the mornings, and having him stay here would mean a curtailment of privacy, she thought worriedly as she dished up Riffy's egg; it would mean remembering to get dressed in the mornings, not having her evenings to herself. What evenings? a mocking voice asked. She didn't get any evenings. Not on her own, anyway. Although Riffy should be going to bed earlier soon, shouldn't she, when she'd finished teething? But it wasn't only that—of course it wasn't only that; he was in the next *bedroom*, and if he ... if she ...

'I'll pay you the same.'

'What? Oh, you don't have to. I mean ...' With a sigh, she sat to feed Riffy her egg. 'It was a lot to start with, wasn't it?'

'I'm sure I'll manage.'

Yes, he looked the sort of man who would be always able to manage—and then she remembered what he had said in the night. And as though he could possibly know what she was talking about she mumbled, 'I hadn't disconnected the baby alarm.'

'You hadn't?'

'No.' She was watching Riffy, not Joshua, and so didn't see his expression, which was probably just as well.

'Butter?'

'What?' Swivelling round, she stared at him, stared at the table. Oh, God. 'In the fridge.' She'd forgotten to get out a fresh packet, which meant it would be hard. 'Sorry. There's marmalade in the cupboard. I think. No Riffy, give me back the spoon, there's a good girl. Thank you,' she muttered as Joshua handed her another one. 'I'm not used to people in the morning,' she added by way of defence. 'I'm not—organised.'

'No,' he agreed. 'Perhaps I'd better take over breakfast whilst I'm here.'

Depressed, feeling diminished, *useless*, she asked, 'Have you ever been married?'

'No.'

'Had little ones to look after?'

'No.'

No, and people who hadn't ever had them didn't understand how difficult it sometimes was. Like juggling with too many balls when you'd never even managed to do it with one. *Some* mornings everything ran smoothly. This didn't happen to be one of them. And non-parents seemed to think you should have a timetable or something, start as you meant to go on, but babies didn't understand timetables... At least, Riffy didn't. And Joshua made her nervous.

'What did you do before you had the baby?' he asked idly.

'Hmm? Oh, interior design...'

He choked, and she looked round in astonishment.

'Sorry,' he managed. 'Crumb went down the wrong way.'

'No, it didn't,' she argued. 'You were laughing!'

'More along the lines of a disbelieving grunt,' he corrected her solemnly, and then glanced pointedly round the kitchen.

'You shouldn't judge by...' she began huffily, then sighed. 'I haven't had the *time*!' Or the money. 'I've only managed to do my bedroom and the nursery, and make the lounge habitable.' The dining room looked as though a pitched battle had been fought and lost in there, the other two bedrooms were dumping grounds for things as yet unsorted, unwanted or awaiting repair, and she began to wonder if she even *noticed* the hall and landing any more. 'I didn't feel in the *least* inadequate until you came,' she retorted crossly. 'And don't *smile*!'

'How do you know I am smiling?'

'I can *feel* it!'

Leaving Riffy to bang with the spoon, she went to heat her milk, *still* avoiding eye contact with him. This was so silly—he was only a *man*, for goodness' sake! And she wished she didn't feel the need to keep filling these awful silences—silences he didn't seem to want to fill, need to fill. And it felt as though they were talking all round a subject that he'd never heard of. Did he know how he made her feel? Yes, of course he did; he probably enjoyed making her feel uncomfortable. And for why? she wondered despairingly. Why pursue her at all?

Not at all confident about her attractiveness to the opposite sex, she couldn't understand what he saw in her. Once she might have done, she thought sadly, but now? No make-up, probably smelling of baby food... And Joshua could probably have any woman he wanted. Women probably fell over, beating a path to his door.

Without looking, she could have told anyone who asked about the little mole beside his left ear, the way his hair grew against his neck, the shape of his eyebrows, his mouth, his nose, the ridged scar on his right thumb... And it was so *stupid*. His body was hard and lean—a body that was worked at to keep it in shape. His teeth were even and white... Jaw gritted, she wrenched her mind violently away.

'How bad was the damage to the cottage?' she demanded abruptly.

'It isn't in immediate danger of collapse, if that's what you were worried about.' He still sounded amused. 'The joists aren't affected, and the roof seems sound, as far as I can tell without actually climbing up there.'

'Oh. And lightning is an exclusion clause, isn't it?' she asked despondently.

'You'd have to check the policy.'

'Mmm.' And even if it covered it she would have to pay a percentage of the claim.

Passing Riffy her bottle with automatic instructions not to dob it everywhere, she made her own toast, poured her own tea, and sat opposite Joshua, eyes lowered, body tense, just as the back door opened and Daniel wheeled himself in.

He halted, stared at them all, and sneered, 'Very cosy. What's *he* doing here?'

Joshua turned his head, looked at him, and greeted him quietly. 'Good morning.'

Daniel flushed, wheeled himself over to Riffy and lay a rather proprietorial hand on her hair. She screwed up her eyes, banged her bottle on the tray and blew a raspberry. Daniel laughed. 'Come on, sweetheart, you don't want to sit in that rotten old chair; come and sit with me.'

'Daniel,' Brogan began tiredly, 'leave her be.'

Ignoring her, he awkwardly lifted her out and sat her on his lap. 'I'll have cereal.'

Avoiding looking at *anyone*, she abandoned her half-eaten toast and went to get his breakfast.

'Did you hear the storm last night?' he asked as he took the bottle from Riffy's hands and began to feed her himself.

'Yes,' Brogan said shortly. Plonking his breakfast at the table, she removed Riffy from his lap and put her back in her high chair, ignored her wail and gave her her bottle. 'Drink.' Much to her astonishment, Riffy broke off mid-wail and put her bottle in her mouth.

With a grunt of surprised laughter, Brogan sat to finish her breakfast. 'It took out the wall of the cottage.'

'What did?' Daniel queried blankly.

'The storm.'

'Brogan—'

'Lightning strike,' Joshua put in laconically. 'Missed me by inches.'

Brogan glanced up, stared at him. He gave her a lazy smile—and a gentle hand squeezed her insides. Hastily averting her eyes, she stared at her plate. No, she thought blankly. Finding him attractive was one thing. *Being* attracted to him was one thing. To have him *promote* that attraction was quite another. Don't smile, she wanted to say. Go back to the eyebrow. The eyebrow is safer. Only, of course, it wasn't. 'Safe' wasn't in that man's vocabulary.

Only vaguely aware that he was explaining the night's events to Daniel, her mind still foolishly trying to find excuses for her feelings, she didn't really register the specific content of his talk until Daniel exclaimed, *'What?'*

Looking up to find Daniel glaring at her, she waited, and he exploded, 'He stayed *here*? In the house?'

'Well, where else was he supposed to stay? In the shed? Of course he stayed here.'

'Are you mad?'

'Not to my knowledge. It was two o'clock in the morning, Daniel!'

'Then you should have *told* me.'

'I'm telling you now.'

'I meant when it happened!'

'Whatever for?'

'Well, if you don't know I'm not going to spell it out!'

'Good.' Irritated, she got up, began to clear the table. 'Do you want any more tea?'

'No.'

'Then go away, both of you; I have things to do. Did you bring your washing in?'

'No,' Daniel said sulkily.

'Then go and get it.'

Joshua gave a small smile, got up and walked out.

'What's amusing him?'

'How would I know?'

'Well, he's your friend.'

'No, he isn't, he's—' Breaking off, she ordered crossly, 'Oh, go away.'

'You're asking for trouble...'

'Go *away*!'

With a mutinous grunt, he wheeled himself out and she saw him catch up with Joshua, say something, saw Joshua reply, then Daniel wheeled himself across to the annexe, a look of bad temper on his thin face.

A few minutes later she saw Joshua go off in his car—a car that looked as beaten up and unreliable as her own—and didn't quite realise how long she stood at the window staring after him, trying to *analyse* him.

She spent the day trying to organise herself, and Daniel, thankfully, stayed out of her way. She inspected the cottage, rang the insurance company, only to be told regretfully that no, her policy didn't cover damage caused by lightning, and so she shoved the matter to the back of her mind. Perhaps Joshua would have some idea how much it would cost to get it repaired. No, she mentally scolded herself, don't ask Joshua, ask a builder; they usually give free estimates.

She managed to get her washing dry before the rain started, which was an on-and-off drizzle, as though it couldn't quite make up its mind what to do. Thunder rumbled menacingly in the distance but didn't come any closer.

She removed the baby alarm from Joshua's room, made the beds, cleaned, polished, made an extra effort with the lounge, made sure the bathroom was spotless, and didn't realise until she heard it that she had been waiting for the sound of his car. And almost—almost—she ran out to greet him. Horrified, she grabbed the bag of potatoes and began to peel them as though her life and her sanity depended on it.

And, as though he too had been waiting, only seconds after Joshua entered the kitchen Daniel followed him, and thereafter, through that long, fraught evening, wherever Joshua was, so too was Daniel. Joshua looked amused. Daniel didn't.

'You don't need to worry, you know,' Joshua drawled provokingly. 'Domesticity bores me.'

'Then go and stay in a hotel!' Daniel said through his teeth. 'You shouldn't *be* here with Brogan on her own!'

'I don't like hotels,' Joshua argued mildly. 'And Brogan needs the money. Don't you, Brogan?'

Brogan didn't answer; she merely walked with as much dignity as she could muster out to the kitchen to make Riffy's last bottle. So domesticity bored him, did it? Tough. And if Daniel didn't stop bitching...

At ten, as though bored with drizzling, the heavens opened. Rain bounced off the roof, overflowed the guttering, probably flattened the corn; the farmers would be cursing, she thought. It pounded the hard-packed earth of the drive until it had pulped it to swamp, pinged viciously off her car, and then, after its burst of spite, an hour later it returned to a spasmodic drizzle.

Joshua read his book, and Brogan and Daniel watched the rain, neither speaking, and if the other two thought profound thoughts Brogan didn't know. She certainly didn't have such thoughts but merely stared blankly, her mind empty.

Not wishing to have to talk, discuss it, she rose abruptly and announced that she was going to bed.

'Lock up after Daniel, would you, Joshua?'

He nodded.

''Night,' she added quietly. As she passed Daniel, he caught her hand, tugged her down, and she obediently kissed his cheek. He'd intended it to be his mouth—she knew it had—for Joshua's benefit. Tiredly shaking her head, she escaped.

To the gentle, almost soothing patter of the rain, she fell asleep almost immediately—and woke abruptly at a violent prod from her subconscious. The dinghy. Oh, God, the dinghy! Flinging the cover aside, she hurtled onto the landing, dragged the loft ladder down with an agonised clang and rapidly climbed. Yanking on the light, she stared.

'Oh, my God,' she whispered.

Galvanised into further action, she slid down, hurtled down to the kitchen, grabbed the bucket and hurtled back up. Out of breath, she dragged herself back into the loft, stumbled over sundry objects, stubbed her toe, cursed, then gently, carefully, bottom lip clenched between her teeth, she eased the bucket into the rubber dinghy, which was full, almost—oh, so nearly—to overflowing.

Water slopped, but not enough to be a danger, and, carefully straightening, shipping water at every step, she carried the bucket to the opening, hovered indecisively, set the bucket down, backed onto the top step and clasped the bucket in her arms. Teeth still mangling her lower lip, she began to descend. Water sloshed down her front and she hissed, grimaced, found another step. Bucket still clasped to her chest, because she had nothing to rest it on in order to transfer it to her hands, and each step a marvel of precision, peripherally aware of Joshua standing in the doorway of his room, she made it to the bathroom and emptied the bucket into the bath.

She hurried back to the ladder and had one foot on the bottom rung when Joshua demanded incredulously, 'What on *earth* are you doing?'

'Can't stop,' she muttered as she scrambled up again. 'But if it doesn't rain all night one more should do it.'

'Do *what*?' he demanded of her disappearing feet. Ascending the ladder behind her, he stared in astonishment at the rubber dinghy in the corner, fully inflated, and full of water.

'Why?' he asked in the dazed voice of a man who knew, really *knew*, that he shouldn't ask.

'Roof leaks,' she mumbled as she carefully eased her bucket into the slopping water.

'Roof leaks,' he repeated flatly. 'Of course it does. What a silly question. Oh, give it to me,' he ordered in a long-suffering voice, 'before you fall in.'

'I have no intention of falling in,' she said with dignity.

'Then before you damage your back! And for goodness' sake go and put some shoes on!' Wrenching the bucket from her, he edged her to one side, and she stared at her bare feet, then at his, then at his face.

He muttered something rude, dragged the bucket out and carried it to the hatch—and descended forwards, bucket held easily in one hand. He didn't stoop, grunt, slop water, give any indication at all that the bucket weighed more than a few ounces.

Full of admiration, absently holding her wet nightie away from her breasts, she stayed where he'd left her, heard him empty the bucket, heard him returning.

'I *knew* there was a reason why women needed men,' she commented admiringly. 'It was just a little difficult to work out what it was. Until now.'

Ignoring her sarcasm, mild as it had been, he demanded, 'How long has this been here?'

'Since we moved in. It's Andrew's... *Was* Andrew's,' she corrected herself, 'when he was a little boy.'

'Well, *surely* it would have been easier to mend the roof?'

'Of course it would,' she agreed, 'but he died before he could do so. And I forgot all about it until now.'

'Then it's a pity you didn't remember *sooner*!'

'And extraordinarily fortunate that I didn't remember *later*!' she exclaimed. 'The dinghy is over your room.'

'Of course. Where else would it be?'

It took him six trips to empty the dinghy, and Brogan perched on a broken chair and watched him, chin in hands. His towelling robe was very short. So was her nightie.

'We really must stop meeting like this,' she quipped.

He ignored her.

With absolutely no idea why she was feeling so unruffled by it all, she continued to watch him. He used an economy of movement that was extraordinarily pleasing—an *efficiency*. Was *this* the real Joshua?

Startled by a thought that had been half-hidden, she frowned. Real? Implying that he was usually acting? Yes, because she did sometimes get the feeling that he was playing a part. On the rare occasions when he was unaware of her watching, his face reverted to sternness, the eyes to coldness, and then he would turn, his expression lightening. Because he didn't want her to know that he had a lot on his mind, was worried about work? Or was it, as Daniel had intimated, because he was playing a part—slumming?

He returned, examined the damp dinghy, glanced at the roof, dumped the bucket, and ordered, 'Bed. Unless there are any more bizarre receptacles waiting to be emptied?'

She shook her head.

'Does Daniel know?'

'Daniel? No,' she denied, puzzled.

'You haven't told him?'

'No. Why would I tell him?'

He shrugged. 'You and your husband both moved in here?'

Still puzzled, not sure where the conversation was heading, or why he had asked, she nodded.

'Well, there's nothing more we can do tonight.' Indicating for her to precede him, he followed her to the loft hatch, yanked off the light and followed her down.

Shoving the ladder back up, he dusted off his hands, stared at her, shook his head, and walked into the bathroom. She heard him wash his hands, watched him emerge and go into his room and quietly close the door. Still puzzled, she finally shrugged, but this Joshua—the Joshua of dinghy fame—was far easier to cope with. No overtly sensual glances, no innuendo... Because he'd forgotten?

His door opened and he looked out. 'Awaiting an invitation?' he asked softly.

'No,' she denied automatically, her face still thoughtful. 'Goodnight, and thank you.'

He nodded, closed his door, and she went quietly into her own room. Checking on Riffy, who slept on undisturbed, she glanced at the clock, was astonished to discover that it was only a little after midnight, climbed into bed—and remembered that tomorrow—today—was Riffy's birthday and she hadn't wrapped her present. She knew that Riffy wouldn't actually *know*, but it still had to be wrapped. Presents always did.

Climbing out again, and without bothering to put on the lights, she padded back downstairs. Carefully opening the dining-room door so as not to make a noise, she groped inside, located the large box and dragged it along to the lounge. She snapped on the table lamp and removed the wrapping paper, sticky tape and scissors from the bureau where she had left them earlier.

Kneeling on the floor, a little smile on her mouth, she began to wrap the box.

'Now what are we doing?' Joshua asked interestedly from the doorway behind her.

Turning her head, she smiled more broadly. 'It's Riffy's birthday.'

'And we get her up now, do we?'

Startled, she laughed, shook her head. 'No, silly. I forgot to wrap her present.'

Leaning one shoulder against the doorframe, he folded his arms across his chest. 'She's one year old, right?'

'Yes.'

'And she *knows* it's her birthday?'

'No, of course not.'

'Then she will not know she has to have a present, will not know it has to be wrapped.'

'But *I* will.'

'Then do it in the morning. I would have thought you get little enough sleep as it is.'

'Don't be silly; she'll see me do it in the morning. It's a surprise. Hold the paper down for me, will you?'

Straightening, he walked across, squatted the other side of the box and obediently held the paper down so that she could tape it.

'What is it?'

'An elephant.' She glanced up, saw his expression and snorted with laughter. 'With wheels and a handle. You think I'm a fool, don't you?'

'Yes.'

'And when you have a family,' she told him gently, 'you'll do exactly the same.'

'Heaven forbid.'

'Don't you want to get married, have children?'

'No.'

No hesitation, no thinking about it, just a flat 'no'—and a little pain curled inside her. She had known—of course she had known—that he didn't want to *marry* her, for goodness' sake, any more than she wanted to marry him, she assured herself, and she'd known that this pursuit was just—flirtation, so why did his words hurt?

'Unless they were special,' he added softly.

Giving him a quick glance, the frown still in her eyes, she absently turned the box, indicated for him to hold the next bit. 'Special?'

'Mmm.'

'And you've not met anyone like that yet?' she asked carefully.

'Stop fishing.'

'I wasn't...didn't...' Abandoning what she was going to say, she taped down the last corner.

'Finished?'

'Yes. I just have to write the label.'

'She can read?' he asked admiringly, and she gave a wry smile, but whether she knew it or not his words had taken the warmth from her eyes, left a trace of sadness.

'It's *important*.' Scrambling to her feet, she found a pen, knelt back down to write.

'"To Riffy,"' he read, '"with lots and lots of love, Mummy."'

'Don't,' she reproved him, her face flushed and suddenly vulnerable. 'I don't care what you think.'

'Not only me.'

'What?'

'I meant, do you care what anyone thinks?'

'Oh. No.' Somewhat confused, she stood, capped the pen, picked up the rest of the paper and scissors, and put them tidily in the bureau.

He stepped up behind her, handed her the tape, and she shivered, felt that little leap of excitement, tried to suppress it, and couldn't. He did excite her, make her yearn for closeness, warmth—all the things her marriage had promised and never delivered. To be able to lean against a strong shoulder, share her worries, her problems... How very defeatist. And that would be *using* him, wouldn't it? And even if it wasn't, if she gave in to these rioting inclinations, when he left, as he undoubtedly would, she would be ten times worse off than now, wouldn't she?

'Why, Joshua?' she asked quietly.

'Why what?' he asked softly, and he was close enough for his breath to stir her hair, feather against her cheek.

'Why the pursuit? I wouldn't have thought I would be at all the sort of woman you'd be attracted to.'

'Who ever knows what attracts?' he asked as he fingered her hair, moved it to one side, touched his mouth to her neck.

With a little shiver, she turned, stared into his face.

'The shape of a nose,' he continued. 'The way they walk, move. Wealth, position, laughter...'

'Wealth?' she asked with a smile. 'I don't have any wealth.'

'No, but one day you might, mightn't you? In a few years.'

'Mmm,' she agreed thoughtfully. She wouldn't always be content to live in this domestic chaos, allow her brain to atrophy; she would want, need to use her talents, and, when Riffy was a bit older, would hopefully start up her business again.

'And Daniel?'

'Daniel?' she queried.

'Mmm. You'll stay with him? Why *do* you stay with him, Brogan?'

Guilt, she was about to say, then changed her mind. 'Because he needs me.'

'And if I needed you?'

'You?' she asked softly and a little sadly, because she couldn't conceive of Joshua ever needing her.

'Would you devote your life to me? What if I were to tell you I was rich?'

'You think that would make a difference?' She smiled, because she didn't believe he was.

'Wouldn't it? If I had a big house? Money in the bank?'

'Do you?'

'Perhaps.'

'And perhaps I'm in line for an inheritance,' she prophesied lightly. 'Then we would both be rich.'

'Yes.'

'But happiness doesn't depend on wealth, does it?'

'What does it depend on, Brogan? An ability to—excite?'

The expression in his eyes, the roughness in his voice said far more than the words, and she felt her breath catch in her throat.

'And we can so easily excite each other, can't we?' Sliding both straps off her shoulders, he pulled her against him, stared down into her wide eyes. 'Can't we?'

Heart jerking unevenly, tape still clutched to her breast, she stared up at him. 'Yes, but that doesn't really explain what I asked.'

'Doesn't it?'

'No. Why me, Joshua?' she demanded huskily. 'If domesticity bores you, why are you trying so hard to seduce me?'

'Do you really not know?'

She shook her head.

'Because I can,' he answered, almost too softly for her to hear.

'What?'

'Touch me,' he ordered, his voice still soft, mesmerising.

'What?'

'Face, arm, hand—anything—because you never do, do you? You carefully avoid contact unless I instigate it. Why?'

'Because...because I don't know what you want from me, and because—I don't have the courage,' she admitted honestly. 'Joshua, it's been a long time since...' She dragged in a deep breath and, eyes still fixed on his, blurted out, 'You sometimes seem to be acting, searching for a response, and I don't...'

Releasing one shoulder, he removed the tape from her, put it behind her on the bureau and slipped both hands round her waist. 'Don't?' he queried softly. 'Don't want to appear—desperate?'

'No!' she denied, horrified.

With a tiny grin—an appealing grin—he touched his nose to hers. 'I am.'

'Am what?' she whispered, confused.

'Desperate.'

'No, you aren't.'

'Don't argue. Kiss me goodnight.'

'Joshua...'

'Or stay in my arms.'

Searching his face—such a strong face, such an unreadable face—she continued to stare up at him in worried confusion.

'Kiss me.'

She touched her mouth to his chin.

'Not good enough.'

With a little groan, firmly suppressing a rising, almost overwhelming desire to do a great deal more than kiss him, aware of the naked body beneath the robe, the strong thighs, the hard chest, she pressed a kiss to his mouth, held her breath to stem the spreading warmth inside as he prolonged it, teased her lips apart, breathed softly into her mouth.

'Now go to bed. It's late. And seduction,' he added softly as he slipped both straps back onto her shoulders, 'can backfire.'

On whom? Feeling dazed, unreal, she switched out the lamp and walked slowly up to her room.

The next day she didn't see him at all. He was up and out before she rose, didn't return until after she was in bed. They had a very nice birthday party without him. With cake. And singing. Daniel bought Riffy too much. Joshua didn't even send her a card. And her exhaustion when she finally went to bed was due to bewilderment, not activity.

She heard him come in, heard him lock the back door. It was late—early in fact. Sunday morning. Sunday. The day of the photoshoot. Oh-h-h... With a fatalistic tut she reached out and set the clock for five.

Staring into the dark, no longer sleepy, she listened to the sounds Joshua made—the tiny creak of the stairs as he ascended, the opening of his bedroom door, the closing, the rustle of clothing removed, the journey to the bathroom, the sound of teeth cleaning. An intimate sound.

And did he look towards her room? Give that odd smile? Expect that any moment she would burst out, *seduce* him? Had he been implying that it was she who'd been trying to seduce him? She didn't know. Or was he wondering at his stupidity in coming to live in a house of chaos—a house where his landlady wandered around in her nightie? And she still didn't know what he *wanted*. His words of the previous night went round and round in her head, and no matter how many times she tried to analyse them, understand them, nothing became any clearer.

Turning her gaze to the wall that separated the two rooms, she continued to think about him, worry about it. Want him.

He would be naked, his robe tossed over the foot of the bed, perhaps, shrugged off when he'd entered his room. Were his hands linked behind his neck? He looked the sort of man who would lie like that. Or was he curled on his side, already asleep? And she wondered how he'd got the scar on his collar-bone. As a child? Falling off his bike, at twelve, thirteen years old, maybe...? She could picture him as a child. Had be been unloved? Unwanted? Was that why he didn't want a family of his own? She would *not* ask.

Brogan, will you go to *sleep*? Perhaps when he'd made that remark about seduction backfiring he'd meant *his* seduction, not hers. But if he'd meant hers then that was insulting. Perhaps women tried to seduce him all the time. He looked like a man who might have had an exciting lifestyle, a man who had once commanded the best... He looked as though he was used to casinos, glittering parties, polo matches or something...

And he made her feel threatened, vulnerable, furious, and aware—oh, yes, so very aware—of her femininity. Only because of the unfamiliarity of having a man in the house, she tried to tell herself. Daniel didn't count as a man, only a friend. Although, the way he was going, they wouldn't even be friends for very much longer. And all those presents for Riffy—a bike which she was too young for, a swing, a Wendy house... Generous—and silly, and she didn't know how to *explain* to him...

If she could just be stronger, she thought for the umpteenth time—more *resolute*... Although, now that the fashion show was over one of the fashion houses would maybe get in touch with him, offer him work, and then he would leave, become independent. That was likely, wasn't it? And then she could maybe start up her business again—just in a

small way to start with—meet new people...
Everything would be all right then, wouldn't it?

Waking with a start, she slapped off the alarm
before it could wake Riffy, or Joshua, and, feeling
totally unrefreshed, totally unlike attending a
fashion shoot, no matter how important, she began
her preparations for a day that would be very long.
And finally, eventually, showered and dressed, Riffy
ready, holdall packed with all her daughter's
necessary bits and pieces, she locked up and walked
round to the annexe to collect Daniel. She did not
even *glance* at Joshua's door.

'Ready?' she asked.

'I suppose.'

'It'll be fine.' Please God, let it be fine.

'It will probably rain.'

'No, it won't; the clouds have gone, and the
forecast said warm and sunny. Any idea how long
it will take?'

He shook his head. 'Not long, I shouldn't think.'

Riffy was strapped into her baby seat, the boot
was carefully loaded with Daniel's collection, the
wheelchair stowed—and the car wouldn't start.

Don't panic, she told herself repeatedly. Don't
flood the engine; just keep calm and try again.
Daniel's hands were bunched on his lap, his face
set.

'Do something!' he gritted.

'I'm trying. It'll be all right—'

'It won't be all right! Well, that's it—I won't
bloody go! All that work, all for nothing... The
photographer won't wait, you know. He's doing it

as a favour. And then the girls will have to be at work—'

'Daniel, calm down; we have plenty of time. I'll ring for a cab—'

'And who's going to pay for the bloody thing? You?'

'Yes, and don't keep swearing. I don't want Riffy's first long words to be profane.'

'Then get this damned car started!'

'I'm trying!'

The back door was yanked open and Joshua strode the few yards towards them. He wore grey trousers and nothing else. Face half-covered in foam, a razor held in one hand, he wrenched open Brogan's door and stared at her. 'What the *hell* is going on now?'

CHAPTER FOUR

'MY LATEST form of seduction,' snapped Brogan.

'It isn't working. And don't you two *ever* stop arguing? What idyllic surroundings, I thought—in the peace and quiet of rural Suffolk. Peace I have yet to find. *Quiet* I have yet to find.'

'You did *not* think that,' she argued. 'You—' Breaking off, belatedly recalling that Daniel was listening, she bit her lip and explained stiltedly, 'The car won't start. Daniel has a photo shoot today, in Lavenham. I'm sorry if we woke you,' she added stiffly.

'You didn't wake me. Do I look as though I shave in my sleep?'

'No, but you sound as though you practise being pithy!'

'I do. Get out,' he ordered. The voice was mild, unemotional, but it was still an order, and there was absolutely *no* amusement in his face this morning.

Mouth set, obeying automatically, she took the razor he handed her and watched him take her place. He turned the key, floored the accelerator—and the battery gave a last whine. He looked as though it was no more than he expected. 'You have jump-leads?' he asked Daniel.

'How would I know? It's not my bloody car.'

He glanced at Brogan, and she shook her head.

'What time do you have to be in Lavenham?'

'Half an hour ago,' Daniel muttered untruthfully.

'I'll ring for a cab,' Brogan repeated.

'Yeah, and by the time it gets here the girls will be at work, the photographer will be gone—'

'Don't be such a pessimist.' Walking back to the house, she halted as Joshua offered, 'I'll drive you.'

Offered? No, it wasn't an offer, it was a statement. 'I don't need you to drive us. I'll get a cab.'

'Get unloaded. I'll be five minutes.'

He returned to the house and within the stipulated five minutes he was back, a short-sleeved navy shirt tidily tucked into clean jeans, face shaved, hair combed, and black moccasins on his feet.

Ignoring them, he walked past, went to get his car. He moved like an athlete—easily, unhurried—despite any mental turmoil. Strong in a supple way, graceful as though he always belonged. Whatever the environment, he was comfortable in it. Her expression indicated a strong desire to carve him into little pieces and feed them to the ducks. A fashion show, her kitchen, a tumbledown country cottage—where else did he feel at home? The unemployment office?

'Brogan!'

'What?' she asked mutinously.

'Unload!'

With an irritable twitch, she retrieved the wheelchair, the collection, her daughter, and within minutes they were transferred to Joshua's car.

'Are you sure it will go?' she asked nastily.

'I'm always sure. Get in.'

Sliding in beside Riffy, she slammed the door, fitted her seat belt into place.

Nobody thanked him.

He climbed behind the wheel, and she glared at his neck, noted the way his thick hair curled across his collar, could see the fingers of his left hand where they steadied the wheel—long fingers, the nails beautifully shaped. She watched the muscles in his forearm flex. A fastidious man, or that was how he seemed. Did he ever laugh, take joy in the morning? Did he even ever *smile*? Yes. But now she didn't know if the smiles had been real.

She wanted to disparage his driving, and couldn't. He was a patient driver, as unemotional behind the wheel as on his feet. She glanced into the rear-view mirror, caught him momentarily watching her, saw the eyebrow go up, and looked quickly away at the hedgerows that lined the lanes, the fields of corn, the mist that still lay on the horizon. She remembered her thoughts in the night. A little sigh diverted her, and she looked across to Riffy strapped in her baby seat and smiled.

'She's asleep?' Daniel asked as he craned his neck round to see.

'Yes.'

'An early start for her.'

'It's always an early start for her,' she said wryly. 'Although, not usually *this* early.'

'No. She's had her breakfast?'

'Of course she's had her breakfast,' she insisted, felt the familiar irritability surface, and forced it down. She didn't want Daniel in the car, didn't want anyone in the car, except maybe Riffy; she would have liked to drive on and on, for days and days, with no need to think or feel, just being. Wouldn't that be nice? she thought.

It was only a ten-minute drive into Lavenham and at Daniel's direction Joshua drove round to the car park behind the market place.

Climbing out, she stared round her at the medieval and Tudor structures that had lasted, with some adaptation, to the present day. It was a beautiful village, with nice people, and, shivering a little in her thin cotton T-shirt, she stared across at the guildhall—built in 1529 when the Guild of Corpus Christi had been granted its charter. And to be used today as a backdrop for the photographs. Appropriate, she supposed—the wool industry had built it, and now the wool industry— well, cloth, apart from her own rubber suit—would use it again. And last week she had trundled a party of tourists round it. Including Joshua. Joshua, who had watched her, excited her, made her nervous. And still did.

The photographer was there checking angles and light, or whatever it was that photographers checked, and four young girls were grouped in the doorway of the guildhall. They looked excited, and Brogan felt very old. Whilst Joshua helped Daniel out and retrieved the collection, she unclipped Riffy, smiled when she woke, gave her a cuddle. 'You be a good girl,' she whispered. 'No tantrums.' Riffy beamed.

Following the others across to the guildhall, she reluctantly handed her daughter to Daniel, then went inside to the room on the right with the other girls to change into the outfits. There was a great deal of giggling and embarrassment.

She'd remembered the talcum powder, but even with that it was still a struggle to get into the tight outfit, a struggle to forget the feel of Joshua's hands as he'd eased her breasts inside the last time she'd worn it, the way his mouth had found her breast the night of the storm... Shut up, Brogan; you're becoming a bore on the subject.

Smothering a yawn, she went outside, and the hour that Brogan had mentally allowed for turned into two as they posed again and again, not only now for the photographer but for the tourists who were beginning to arrive, the people who worked in the shops, the information centre, and Brogan was grateful for the helmet which at least partially concealed her features.

And the photographer was merciless. Stand here, do that, smile, stretch, jump—jump? They were shouted at, prodded, pushed into unnatural postures until he ran out of film, and Brogan began to hope that that was it, that they could all go home.

Once, not so long ago, she would have enjoyed all this, laughed with the other girls, entered into the spirit of the thing, and didn't really know why she couldn't. Because Joshua was watching? Was that it? Because she felt intimidated? A fool? Angry? The sun was beginning to touch the market place and, as uncomfortable as she was now, soon it would get much worse.

Daniel, the photographer and the other girls were in a group in the middle of the square—almost as if Riffy was holding court, Brogan thought with a smile. Certainly she was enjoying all the attention. One of the girls was giving her her bottle, and Brogan felt a momentary stab of jealousy, and then became aware of Joshua at her side. Giving him a look of dislike, expecting to see impatience or irritation on his strong face, she found it as expressionless as ever.

'It's taking longer than expected,' she muttered, an apology that was in no way apologetic.

'Not your fault.'

Astonished, she stared at him, her grey eyes wide.

He gave an odd smile. 'You expected me to blame you?'

'Why not? You've blamed me for everything else.'

'Nonsense.'

Nonsense? *Nonsense?* 'Have a faulty memory, do you?'

His smile widened. 'We *are* grouchy this morning.' Nodding towards Daniel, he added, 'He seems to be enjoying himself for once.'

'Yes.'

'Like your daughter, he likes to be the centre of attention.'

'Yes.' And it was true. He'd always been rather intense, serious, but he'd liked to be in the thick of things, be—important, and a wave of guilt washed over her, because Daniel's present condition was her fault.

One of the girls came across, grinned at Brogan, gave Joshua a flirtatious glance and asked curiously, 'What happened to Daniel?'

'I did,' Brogan said quietly. 'Have we finished?'

The girl looked a bit startled, glanced at Joshua as though seeking help or confirmation, then nodded. 'Yes, we can get changed now.'

'Good.' Turning, she hurried, or tried to, back into the guildhall and began to change into her cotton trousers and T-shirt. She wished her thoughts could be changed so easily, then apologised rather shamefacedly to the young girl who followed her in. 'Sorry, I didn't mean to be short with you. It's this outfit—makes me bad-tempered.'

'I'm not surprised.' She smiled. 'I'm glad I didn't have to force myself into it.'

'No. He was in a car crash,' Brogan explained reluctantly, feeling, after her rudeness, that she owed the girl some sort of explanation. 'I was driving.'

'Oh, poor you.'

Surprised, she queried, 'Poor me?'

'Yes, of course; you must feel so wretched about it. Poor Daniel too, of course, but don't you think that sometimes physical hurts are easier to deal with than mental ones?'

'Yes,' Brogan agreed, surprised by the young girl's maturity. Thoughtfully collecting her holdall, she went outside. Daniel was still the centre of attention.

Retrieving her daughter, she said quietly to him, 'I'll meet you back at the car.'

'Where are you going?'

'Just for a walk.'

'Well, don't be long. You can leave the baby with me.'

'Don't be so—peremptory. I'll see you later.' Hoisting her daughter into a more comfortable position, she added, 'It will be a few minutes before the collection's packed up again.'

Without waiting for an answer, or another argument, she walked off down Lady Street, and wondered at her need to keep explaining things to him. She didn't need to justify her action in taking her own daughter. She didn't need to justify her actions to anyone.

'Feeling better?' Joshua asked as he fell into step beside her.

'No.'

'More nocturnal ramblings?'

'No.'

'How did the party go?'

'Fine.'

'Did she like her elephant?' he persevered.

'Yes.'

'No more leaks?'

'No.'

'I'll have a look at the roof when we get back if you like.'

Halting abruptly, she turned to face him, stared into a face that gave nothing away—into eyes that were hatefully bland.

'I was *not* trying to seduce you!'

The eyebrow went up, and his lips twitched. Involuntarily, she was sure.

'And I don't need you to look at the roof.'

'You've mended it?'

'No.'

'Then I need to look at it.'

'Why?'

'Self-preservation? And I was not accusing you of trying to seduce me,' he added softly.

'Yes, you were. You said—'

'I was teasing.'

She stared at him. He stared blandly back. 'Take your tongue out of your cheek, Joshua,' she warned. 'Teasing is the one thing I won't accept.'

'You don't like being teased?' he asked lightly.

'I don't *believe* you were teasing.'

Looking hatefully amused, he changed the subject. 'Did you ring the insurance company?'

'Yes. It isn't covered.' Halting for no particular reason other than that Riffy was getting heavy and she felt she'd walked far enough, she stared rather fixedly at the priory.

'Thirteenth-century hall house,' he commented.

'I know.'

'Fine examples of pargeting.'

She snorted.

'The raised plaster decoration,' he explained.

'*I* know what pargeting is.'

'Do you?'

'No,' she confessed, then gave him a sideways look. '*Were* you teasing?'

'Mmm.'

'Oh, well, all right.'

'It's beautifully restored inside. Medieval and Jacobean staircases, Tudor brick fireplace, cross beams and crown-post roofs...'

'I *know* all this, Joshua. *I* told *you*.'

'So you did. Five days and seventeen hours ago,' he added even more softly.

Looking down, straightening the collar of Riffy's dress, she sighed. 'Wish I had them,' she murmured. 'Then I could open my house to the public.'

'Put your daughter on display. She'd knock 'em dead.'

Glancing at Riffy, to see that she was staring at Joshua with one of her best expressions, she laughed. 'Wretched child.'

'You don't mean that.'

'No.'

'Here, give her to me; she's too heavy for you. You should have brought the pushchair.'

'Probably. And I didn't think you liked babies.'

'I don't like *wet* babies.'

'Or one of your own.'

The sound he made was decidedly noncommittal, and then Riffy took the decision out of her hands anyway. She lunged at Joshua, and he caught hold, hoisted her into his arms, watched her face as though he, too, were fascinated—or just curious as to what made her tick.

'Why the sudden desire for conversation?' she asked quietly.

'Curiosity.' Still looking down into the baby's face—a face that was being artfully expressive—he chuckled.

Still trying to come to terms with the chuckle, Brogan asked absently, 'About what?'

'You.'

'Why?'

He smiled, glanced at her. 'Do you question *everything*?'

'Yes. No. You make me nervous.'

'Good. Time to go back.' Turning, he waited, then walked with her back up the hill.

Good? Why was making her nervous good?

'Is that why you were so foul? To make me nervous?'

'I'm never foul,' he contradicted her mildly.

Exasperated, she hurried to keep up with his long strides. 'I don't know anything about you,' she stated somewhat breathlessly. 'And don't walk so fast.'

He slowed. 'Belated realisation that you have a stranger in your house? Worry not; I've neither raped nor pillaged.'

'It isn't belated,' she argued. 'Is the job going well? Is that why you were out all day yesterday?'

He hesitated. 'Tender,' he corrected her, 'not job.'

'But a good possibility that your design will be accepted?'

He nodded—almost cautiously, she thought.

'Oh, I *am* glad.'

'Are you?' And now he sounded surprised, she thought.

'Yes, of course. It must have been wretched having no work. And you aren't used to...'

'Pigging it?' he suggested carefully, and she laughed.

'No—at least, you don't look as though you are. You look—expensive.'

His smile was rueful.

'Are you? Were you?'

'Something like that,' he agreed.

'And is that why you said all those things about wealth?'

'Possibly.'

'Joshua! Don't be so aggravating!'

He smiled. 'Tell me about you.'

'Tell you what?'

'Anything. Everything.'

'There's nothing to tell,' she denied awkwardly. 'What you see is what you get.'

He grunted with laughter. 'Then heaven help us all.'

'Yes, well...' Emerging back into the square, she saw that Daniel was still holding court. He waved them over, then explained, 'I'm staying for a bit. I'll see you later.'

Surprised, unconcerned, still in fact turning Joshua's last words over in her mind, she nodded, walked on towards the car, then belatedly wondered if he assumed that Joshua would wait for him. 'I can get a cab back...' she began.

'No need. One of the girls will run Daniel back.' Joshua competently fitted Riffy into her seat, checked the straps, then held the front passenger door open for Brogan.

Climbing in, she fitted her seat belt in place, stared from the window. Heaven help them all? Because of the dinghy, did he mean? Her disorganisation? And something had changed between them, but she didn't quite know what.

'What are you so busily thinking about?' he asked quietly. He no longer sounded amused.

'Hmm? Oh, nothing much. What to have for lunch, I expect.'

He didn't look as though he believed her.

Pulling up behind the house, he unclipped Riffy and handed her to Brogan, took something from the rear shelf, then locked the car.

Holding up what he'd retrieved, he smiled and explained, 'Receipt book. Have to keep everything—above board, don't we? I've filled in the first rent receipt; all you need to do is sign it.' He took the back doorkey from her, used it, ushered her inside.

Passing Riffy to him without thinking, she found a pen and quickly signed the receipt. Tearing it out, she gave it to him. He gave her the rest of the rent in exchange.

'No need to look so worried.'

'I wasn't aware I was.'

'A cold drink? Tea? Coffee?'

'Yes, of course. I'll make it.'

A faint smile leaked into his eyes as he explained, 'I was offering.'

'Oh.'

'Sit in the garden,' he ordered mildly. 'I'll make some tea. Sugar?'

'Two.'

Feeling mindless, confused, she did as she was told, sank onto one of the rickety chairs that sat at an equally rickety table. Rustic, she reproved herself, not rickety. And why on earth had he offered to make her tea? Did she look as though she needed it?

Riffy wriggled to get down and she put her on the grass, remembered the rain they'd had, and fetched an old blanket from the shed. Giving her some toys to play with which might keep her occupied for *five* minutes, she resumed her seat, absently watched her daughter as she contentedly put a brick inside a plastic bucket and took it out again, a look of absorption on her face.

Why the sudden friendliness? He'd flirted with her, aroused her, but he hadn't exactly been friendly, had he? So why now? Because he felt *sorry* for her? And she sometimes got the feeling that he promoted conversations that held no interest for him.

He came out, put two cups on the table and murmured, 'I'll open up the cottage, take a look at the damage.'

She nodded, turned to watch him walk across the grass—lithe and co-ordinated, totally in control. A man who had once been wealthy? And hoped to be again, now that he had a chance of a job? Perhaps that was all his behaviour had been—worry over not working.

He opened the cottage door, wedged it wide, and she could see an open briefcase sitting on the desk, papers scattered. An architect's board stood in one corner, a drawing pinned to the surface, an anglepoise lamp fixed to the bookshelf to one side so that the light would fall on his work—work he was hoping someone might accept? The windows were flung wide to let in some fresh air, and then he was back. He smiled, took the seat opposite, reached for his tea. 'It's not too bad. I'll get someone to fetch over some building materials, patch it for you.'

'Oh, you don't need—'

'Don't I?' he smiled. 'Do it yourself, can you?'

With a wry smile, she shook her head. 'Thank you. I'll—'

'Don't offer to pay me,' he interrupted drily.

'Oh, well, thanks.' With a funny little grimace, part embarrassment, part confusion, she added, 'Tell me about being an historical architect. What exactly is it that you do?'

'Conservation work mostly for the Building Preservation Trust.'

'Only there's not much about at the moment?'

Again there was that hesitation before he shook his head.

'You said something about a Norman villa.'

'Keep. Or it was, once upon a time.'

'And you're hoping to help rebuild it?'

'Re-create it.'

With a faint smile, gradually relaxing, feeling surprisingly unthreatened for the first time in their acquaintanceship, she asked, 'Are you always this pedantic?'

'Always. Drink your tea.'

With another faint smile, glancing down, she lifted her cup and sipped.

'What about Daniel's parents?' he asked idly. 'Do they come to see him?'

Why this abnormal interest in Daniel? she wondered. Everything they discussed, talked about, always came back to Daniel. 'No,' she denied. 'He said he doesn't get on with them, that they fuss. I saw them at the hospital,' she added quietly, 'after the accident. They were quite elderly. I tried to talk to them, tell them how sorry I was...'

With a distressed little sound, she finally continued, 'They were angry, confused, hating me. And who could blame them? I haven't seen them since. I did write, but—' Breaking off, she watched as Riffy abandoned her game and was off across the grass like a bear scenting an unexpected cache of honey. The child grabbed Joshua's leg, hauled herself up, scrambled onto his lap, and then sat there beaming.

'No taste?' he asked softly, and Brogan smiled.

'She likes men. Have to keep an eye on her when she's older.'

'Mmm. Why Poryphia?'

'Oh, Andrew always wanted a little girl, always said that if we had one that's what he would like her to be called. It's from a poem, I think, only not actually Poryphia,' she added with an appealing little laugh. 'It's supposed to be Porphyria, but the registrar came round the ward before I was properly awake and between my wooziness and his confusion it got misspelled.'

'So Poryphia it is.'

'Mmm.'

'And porphyry is also a geological term for various igneous rocks with large, conspicuous crystals in a fine-grained, ground mass.'

Staring at him in astonishment, she burst out laughing. 'I don't think Andrew knew *that*!'

'Doesn't seem likely, does it?'

'No, and she'll have your buttons off,' she warned as Riffy balanced herself upright and began trying to peer down the front of his shirt.

He smiled, clasped the two tiny hands, put them against his mouth, then, to Riffy's delight, blew a raspberry into her palms. She chortled, jumped, and he grunted. With a rather rueful smile—a smile that Brogan found extraordinarily appealing—he lifted her, walked across to the cottage, collected a magazine, and returned. 'I don't suppose she'll mind that it doesn't have lions and tigers in it, only old buildings.'

'No, she isn't in the least discriminating when it comes to something she can eat,' Brogan said drily as Riffy tore off a page and began to push it into her mouth.

He hastily retrieved it, and instead of looking helpless, passing her back as Brogan had half expected he looked round for something else that would distract her. Riffy beat him to it and lunged for his cup.

'Uh-uh-uh.' Hastily whipping it out of her reach, he laughed, and Brogan handed him the bucket that Riffy had been playing with earlier, which Riffy promptly put on her head and proceeded to play peek-a-boo with.

'Is she like this *all* the time?'

'Except when she's asleep, yes. She's getting hungry, I expect. I'd better go and do her lunch.' Yet she stayed where she was, feeling extraordinarily reluctant to actually move. He was different today, softer somehow, and without her quite realising it the awareness she felt was turning to something else.

Still watching him as he continued to amuse her daughter, hypersensitive to his moods, she admired the play of muscles in his strong body when he moved, the way the sun highlighted his dark hair, made fascinating angles on his face, and such an ache of loneliness flooded her that she got quickly to her feet.

He looked up at her, his eyes direct, unwavering, and she felt that funny little pain that started in her throat and plunged to her stomach. Unable to look away, unable to interpret the expression in those dark, dark eyes, she was drawn into a moment of suspension, a moment when everything suddenly stopped, when peripheral sounds were crystal-clear—the buzz of a fly, the drone of a distant aircraft, her own quiet breathing—and then Riffy threw the bucket and real time resumed.

With a blink, not quite sure what had happened, she reached for her daughter, mumbled something and fled. Feeling exposed, she hurried into the kitchen. Nothing had happened, and yet it felt as though they had made love. Crazy.

Fitting Riffy into her high chair, Brogan set about getting their lunch, but her mind wouldn't leave it alone—the look of him, the way she had felt, the yearning for something more—to love and be loved, to *express* that love. Fully, completely, passionately. Andrew had not been passionate and she'd had to suppress her own feelings, pretend that she had not minded. Yet why? Why had she pretended, almost as though such feelings were shameful? She did not know.

She jumped when he came up behind her, stiffened, but he merely passed her and said casually, 'I'll take a look at the hole in the roof.'

'Thank you,' she whispered. 'Joshua?' she called urgently, and when he halted asked lamely, 'Shall you want any lunch?'

He shook his head. 'I'll get myself something later.'

By the time she and Riffy had eaten, he had finished the roof and was over at the cottage—working, she supposed, or examining the damage. When she'd given Riffy her bottle, she put her outside in her pram for her nap, and, collecting some sewing, she settled herself outside in the shade—and deliberately placed her lounger so that her back would be towards the cottage. But she knew he was there, knew he might be watching, and it made her nervous.

With a sigh, she forced herself to concentrate on sewing patches onto the knees of a pair of Riffy's dungarees. It would be silly to buy new ones when these would last until she began walking, which wouldn't be long. She'd already managed one or two wobbly steps. Finding that her mind was wandering, that it was really too hot to concentrate on sewing, she let the dungarees lie in her lap, allowed her thoughts to wander, allowed the silence and the warmth to drift over her.

Still tired from too many broken nights, Brogan closed her eyes, and in that state of half sleeping, half waking became aware that she was no longer alone. Lazily opening her eyes, she stared up at Joshua. He smiled, and, her face flushed and sleepy, she smiled back.

'Too hot to work,' he stated softly.

'Yes.' He'd unbuttoned his shirt, allowed it to lie outside his trousers. His feet were bare. Long feet, narrow, elegant—if feet could ever be said to be elegant. He sat, rested his back against her lounger, linked his hands across his updrawn knees and she stared at his hair, at the way it curled across his neck, wanted to reach out and touch, curled her hand in on itself in denial. It felt like such a long time since she had touched a man intimately, been touched in return, and a flood of warmth entered her stomach, tightened her thighs.

'Did you always want to be an interior designer?' he asked lazily. 'Always want to do something artistic?'

'Artistic?' she queried, and again it felt as though they were talking all round another subject—an intimate subject. Trying to concentrate, ignore it, she replied, 'I don't know that I'd call it artistic having a good eye for colour, design.'

'Never wanted to paint? Sculpt?'

'Paint?' How odd he should think that, because she *had*. Had been quite good at it. Even had an O level in it. 'What made you ask?'

'The way you move, touch things. Long-fingered hands,' he explained softly, half turning his head so that he could see them. 'A deliberation about what you do.'

'Is there? Do I?' she asked stupidly. Flattered, obscurely pleased, she gave a little smile, funny and appealing. Wistful. 'I did paint,' she confessed.

'Then why change?' Shifting slightly, turning his head the other way so that he could see her face, he waited.

Looking down, almost afraid to meet his eyes, her little smile still in place, she shook her head. 'Oh, not much money in it. I had my own business,' she added in an endearing little boast.

She had sometimes wondered if Andrew hadn't courted her because of her business. He would have done up the outside of houses, she would have done up the inside. Only, he'd never had time to do up the outside of the first project they'd begun. And now she had no time to do up the inside. But she had liked to paint—the absorption, the concentration, creating light and warmth and colour, the satisfaction she had gained when she'd done something *good*.

Glancing up, registering the expression on his face, her smile slowly died. Eyes so dark, lashes thick, his skin warm-looking, lightly tanned, the mouth such a beautiful shape—and the groan started without her awareness, rose, was almost allowed its freedom, and if she shuffled down the lounger just a fraction her face would be level with his, their cheeks would touch, warm skin against hers...

He reached up, slowly, without haste or urgency, touched his fingers to her mouth, trailed his thumb across her lower lip, back and forth, his eyes on his task; he changed to a downward movement so that her lips parted, then he touched his index finger inside her mouth, and that delicious warmth spread through her, made her ache, and without being fully aware what she did she licked his fingertip, gripped it gently between her teeth, and his other hand moved to her arm, her shoulder, gently urged her forward to cover the small distance between them, and as his fingers were replaced by his mouth she felt a jolt go through her, an almost physical pain of desire, want, need—and the groan was finally born. And he did want to be touched, didn't he? He'd said so.

Her hands still lay in her lap, curled loosely, and yet it felt the hardest thing in the world to move them, hesitantly touch his neck below his ear, slide her fingers into that thick hair. He shifted slightly and her own hair slipped free, spread to cover his hand as he continued the gentle exploration of her mouth, tasted her with his tongue, just softly, cautiously, allowing her to draw back if she wanted. She didn't want. Dream time, she thought hazily. Warm and special and drifting . . .

Her hand found its way inside his collar, slid dreamily round to the front, to his collar-bone, his chest, brushed his nipple, and the excitement spread. Her other hand found his waist, the hard, flat stomach, the barrier of his waistband, and the kiss deepened, became urgent.

She didn't hear the car, didn't hear the voices, didn't hear anything, feel anything except the mouth moving on hers, warm fingers on her nape, her arm, her breast, but Joshua did, and he gently broke the contact, smiled at her, rose lithely to his feet.

'I'll go and ring the builders' merchants.'

Shaken, barely aware of what he'd said, still able to feel his touch, his mouth, she blinked dazedly when Daniel wheeled himself round the corner, halted beside her, and before she could stop him,

before she could register his intent he kissed her
full on the mouth—a mouth that still held the im-
print of Joshua's.

Jerking back, she exclaimed, 'No! What *do* you
think you're doing?' An overreaction, she knew,
but she could hardly explain why. 'You shouldn't
kiss me,' she muttered.

'Why?' he demanded. 'Because Joshua's
watching? You don't need to worry about *him*! Or
do you?' he asked suspiciously.

'No,' she denied thickly. Was he watching? Not
sure if she wanted to know, she got unsteadily to
her feet, walked over to the pram, saw that Riffy
was awake and made an unnecessary to-do of un-
doing the straps, picking her up.

'You don't need to pretend,' he said sulkily. 'And
you've never objected before.' And all was said loud
enough for Joshua to hear.

Disbelief at his casual lie making her voice harsh,
she said, 'I don't pretend for anybody.'

He shrugged. 'I'll take the baby—'

'You will not take the baby. You will go away
and leave me in peace.'

Riffy shrieked—a high-pitched sound that always
made Brogan wince, a sound that her daughter delighted in—and before Brogan could stop her she
was out of her arms and onto Daniel's lap. Daniel
smirked and wheeled himself inside.

She took a deep breath, held it, counted to ten,
then slowly released it. Let it lie, she told herself;
just let it lie. No. She'd been letting it lie too long.
They needed to talk. Really talk. She had to make
him understand that this—pretence had to end, that

she had her own life to lead—a life she must be *allowed* to lead. She would probably always feel guilty about the accident, but guilt must not be allowed to make her his emotional slave. She did not love him, had never loved him, had only ever thought of him as a friend. He *knew* that, and so this *protection* must end. Now.

Straightening her shoulders, she took a resolute little breath and followed him. 'Daniel . . .'

He turned, grinned, and she felt an overwhelming desire to hit him.

'Mac invited me to stay with him,' he said cheerfully.

'Mac?'

'The photographer. He's got some really excellent ideas for promotion. Ground-floor flat—'

'Then why don't you go?'

'Nah, can't leave you and my babe, can I, sweetheart?' he asked Riffy.

'She isn't your babe, and of course you can leave us. It will do you good.'

'You *want* me to go?'

'Yes,' she said quietly after the smallest of hesitations. 'I think we need a break from each other. We've been living in each other's pockets for weeks . . .' Say it, she urged herself; say it all, now, whilst you have the chance. 'I—'

'Really?'

'What?' she asked, momentarily confused.

'You really want me to go?' Looking suddenly thoughtful, he nodded. 'OK.'

'What?'

'Joshua will have to go as well, of course. I'll go and tell him.'

'No!' Suddenly aware of how urgent she'd sounded, she tried to look casual, and managed to say quietly, 'Why does Joshua need to go?'

'He can't stay here with you on your own.'

'Why not? It's not a problem. Anyway, he's fixing up the cottage—he'll be able to move back. And I need the money.'

Staring at her suspiciously, he demanded, 'No other reason?'

'Of course not.' Glad he could not see the furious beating of her heart, the pulse that hammered in her neck, she turned away, and added casually, 'What other reason could there be?'

CHAPTER FIVE

'YOU really think you need some time on your own?' he repeated quietly.

'Yes. This last year... Daniel, I owe you a lot, but I owe myself something too. It's still all scrambled up in my head. Andrew, the baby, the accident...'

'And I've been trying to rush things. Mac said something like that. OK,' he said again. 'I'll go for a week; it could be really useful for me too. I can get my portfolio together. I'll leave you his number. If anyone rings—you know...'

'Fashion houses, agents... Yes, of course.' Coward, she castigated herself; his 'trying to rush things' sounded as though he thought that there would be a chance for him later, and there wouldn't—he must *know* that. But, desperate for him to go, fighting not to sound too eager, too hopeful, she allowed the cowardice to continue as she added encouragingly, 'It will be good for us both.'

He was watching her carefully, steadily, as though trying to read her mind—or trying to catch her out in a half-truth. And so she smiled, felt a wave of relief wash over her when he nodded.

'Amanda said she would pick me up, run me to his flat. He lives in Bury St Edmunds. Not far. If you need me...'

'Yes. I'll ring.'

An hour later, he was packed and ready to go, only awaiting Amanda.

'You are sure?' he asked for the tenth time.

'Yes.'

'And you'll be able to manage?'

'Yes. That sounds like a car,' she added thankfully.

'I can always change my mind—'

'No. The break will do us good.' And maybe he would discover that he no longer needed her, that Amanda was younger, prettier, that Mac could further his burgeoning career.

'OK. Kiss me goodbye.'

Aware of Amanda in her van, of Joshua in the cottage, she bent, kissed him lightly on the nose— and he grabbed her, one surprisingly strong hand on her neck, forced her face to remain close, and kissed her hard on the mouth.

'I've had a word with Joshua. If you have any trouble with him...'

'I won't. Go.'

And still he lingered.

'I'll see you next week.'

'Yes. Take care.' Afraid that even now he would change his mind, she broke contact, walked across to Amanda's van, opened her door and smiled.

'This is kind of you.'

Amanda grinned, shrugged. 'I don't mind. He's all ready?'

'Yes. I'll give you a hand to load up.'

'Thanks.'

Amanda settled Daniel in the passenger seat, joined Brogan at the rear and hoisted in his wheelchair. 'Are you and Daniel...' she began awkwardly. 'Er...'

'No,' Brogan denied quietly. 'Just friends. Truly. I know he sometimes behaves as though it were more, but it isn't, honestly. He's just a bit proprietorial sometimes. He was a friend of my husband.'

'Oh, right.' She grinned, slammed the rear doors and hurried round to the driver's side. She winked at Brogan, started the engine and bumped slowly back to the road.

She would be alone with Joshua. It should have worried her. It didn't. Anticipation, perhaps foolish, warmed her stomach, tightened her throat. Half-formed needs clouded her mind—needs she tried to dismiss, ignore; but her body felt different already—fuller, softer—and there was an ache in her heart, behind her eyes. Who would it hurt? Only herself.

'I thought he would never go,' Joshua said softly from behind her, and his breath stirred her hair, put tension in her shoulders.

'What did he say to you?' she whispered huskily.

'To leave you alone.'

And are you going to? she wanted to ask. But she didn't quite dare.

One long finger touched the cord in her neck, and she shivered, wanted to turn, be held, but she stayed still, hardly breathing.

'Why don't we eat out tonight?' he asked even more softly.

'Out?' she repeated, as though she'd never heard of such a thing.

'Mmm, you know, posh frocks, candlelight.'

'Candlelight?'

'Mmm.'

'What about Riffy?'

'What about her?'

'I don't have a babysitter or anything.'

'Then we'll take her with us.'

'Take her?' she echoed. A blackbird was sitting on the handle of the fork, watching her, head tilted; Riffy was staggering round and round the patchy grass hanging grimly onto the handle of elephant. She sounded as though she was talking to herself, giving herself instructions, and Brogan smiled, stayed perfectly still.

Raising her eyes slightly, she watched the trees that edged the farmer's field gently sway, and the sky was blue, hard, bright, and it felt as though she wouldn't be able to take a deep breath ever again, or that if she did everything would shatter.

'And, delightful as your back is,' he breathed softly, 'I would much prefer to have this conversation face to face.' Touching her shoulder, he gently turned her, left his fingers lying against her nape. 'Look at me.'

She lifted her lashes, felt dizzy.

'Did your husband never take you out for dinner?'

'Andrew? No.'

'You don't like going out to dine?'

'Yes. I mean...' Andrew had never asked her; Andrew had always said it was a waste of money—and Andrew had always thought that whatever he decided would be fine with her. And mostly it had been. He'd been prosaic, unperceptive, hard-working, in control. Yet she had loved him. She hadn't known him very well, but she had loved him, hadn't she? But talking to him had never made her feel like this. Barely touching had never made her feel like this.

'You have something to wear?'

She nodded, shook her head, despaired at her lack of sophistication. 'Yes, of course.'

He smiled. 'Are you always this confused?'

'No.' Only with you, she added silently.

He trailed his fingers round to her jaw, withdrew them, lightly tapped her nose with one long forefinger. 'Seven.'

She nodded, watched him walk back to the cottage. Oh, Brogan, she thought. 'Joshua?' she suddenly called, and when he turned, asked worriedly, 'Can you afford it?'

'Yes,' he said quietly.

Was he living on his savings? She didn't want him to use his savings.

'I could cook something...'

'Er...no,' he said.

'I can cook!'

'Mmm. Seven,' he repeated, and walked away.

I can cook, she thought indignantly. It might not be cordon bleu...

* * *

She changed, changed again, hated herself, wanted to look nice for him, wanted to look *special*. This was absurd. She'd do better not to go. He was taking her to dine, giving her a treat. Probably because he felt sorry for her. Pull yourself together, Brogan.

Glancing in the mirror at her daughter perched in the centre of the bed playing with some beads, she smiled. Riffy looked nice. She was wearing her best white dress and matching knickers, with white frilly socks which, amazingly, she had left on. She was still clean, but not for much longer if Brogan didn't get a move on. Brogan flicked a glance at the clock. Ten minutes left.

Wrenching off the black dress, hurling it into the corner, she changed her underwear from black to cream, pulled the cream linen dress over her head, zipped it up, defiantly shoved her feet into her tan high-heeled sandals, tipped everything out of her black bag, found the tan one, shoved it all in, found a long multicoloured scarf, wound it round her throat, ignored her reflection, shoved bottle, spare nappy and baby wipes into her bag, picked up Riffy and walked out. If he didn't like the way she looked . . .

She felt exhausted.

She marched into the kitchen and halted. He looked—lovely. With a little grunt of laughter at her terminology, she changed that to terrific. Navy suit, the jacket draped over one of the chairs, well-cut trousers, dark blue shirt, expensive tie with blue and pink and grey swirls. His glance was equally comprehensive, but whether her appearance pleased him or not she didn't know, was unable to tell from his expression, and defiantly told herself that she didn't care one way or the other. But she did. Wanted to ask. Forced herself not to.

'You look nice,' she said brightly.

The eyebrow quirked slightly, and he smiled, looked amused. 'Would you like me to carry Riffy?'

'She'll probably dribble down you.'

'It doesn't matter.' He took her, held her easily in his arms, asked Brogan to bring his jacket and walked out, leaving her to lock the cottage.

'Did you put your battery on charge?' he asked as he opened the rear door of his car and fitted Riffy into the seat which was still there from this morning. Her silence was all the answer he needed. 'I'll do it when we get back.' He didn't sound cross or impatient, just—accepting, as though he expected nothing less, and that made her irritable. Again.

'*I'll* do it when we get back,' she argued.

He smiled, opened the passenger door for her, closed it behind her and walked slowly round to his own seat. 'You look very nice,' he praised her softly as he fired the engine.

'Thank you,' she said tartly, and he laughed.

'Does your bedroom look like a hurricane passed through it?'

Giving him a startled glance, not sure whether to be cross, indignant or amused, she settled for amusement. 'Yes. Know a lot of women, do you? Know their ways?'

'Mmm.'

Out of your depth here, Brogan, she thought. Best buy some wellingtons. Or waders. Yes. Best to go down fighting. She glanced back at Riffy, glanced at Joshua, glanced to the front, and shook her head. 'Where are we going?'

'Other side of Long Melford. Italian. You like Italian food?'

Bit late to ask if she didn't. 'Yes.'

He flicked her a glance, laughed. 'Against expectations, I think I quite like you, Brogan Carpenter.'

'Thank you,' she said primly. 'I'm not sure I like you.'

This time his laugh was longer, and much more genuine. 'Relax. I promise to give you a good time.'

'I'm already quaking. And what do you mean, "expectations"?' she demanded. 'Expectation implies—'

'Implies that attraction does not always indicate liking,' he interrupted her smoothly.

She wasn't sure that she believed his glib explanation. Yet what other one could there be?

The restaurant looked, felt, behaved as though it had been transported lock, stock and barrel from Italy. And, true to his promise, Joshua gave Riffy and her a very good time. He was obviously well-known, and was greeted like an old friend. The baby was taken away to be admired by the kitchen staff, the owner's wife, the waitresses—and half the patrons as well. Riffy loved it all—the attention, the laughter, the exclamations—and Brogan felt proud. That's what she liked about the other Europeans—

they liked babies, accepted them in their res-
taurants. The English usually looked disapproving.

The food was excellent, the wine delicious, and
if she had a little too much no one was counting.
Joshua was charming, amusing, delightful, and, if
a tiny, cynical part of her mind kept asking why,
she had no trouble in ignoring it. Live for the day.
Even if it was all a pretence on Joshua's part, even
if he was behaving like this out of boredom, or
amusement, or pity, she didn't care. It had been a
long, long time since she had felt so special. So
attractive.

Rusty skills re-emerged—a gentle wit, a fund of
long-forgotten stories. And their laughter,
amusement was heady stuff to a girl who had had
nearly two years of nightmare, grief and too little
sleep. She felt relaxed and happy and didn't want
to go home.

They did, of course, and the wine still running
in her veins made her bold. He waited on the
landing whilst she put a sleeping Riffy to bed, and,
excitement, warmth, happiness suffusing her face,
she returned to stand in front of him, slide her arms
round his neck and press a kiss to his chin.

'Thank you. I've had a lovely time.'

'And is the lovely time now over?' he asked softly
as he linked his arms loosely round her waist, drew
her closer so that their bodies touched.

Eyes wide, thought suspended, a sliding pain in
her tummy, she just stared at him.

'Is it?' he insisted, his voice barely audible. He
bent his head, teased her lips apart, slid his tongue

briefly inside, ran it across her front teeth. 'You taste of wine and a promise of pleasure to come.'

And it felt so good to be held like this, touched like this—so safe and warm and special. Resting her head on his shoulder, she closed her eyes, savoured the peace of it, the feel of him, the gentle rise and fall of his chest.

'Gone to sleep?' he teased, and she shook her head.

He removed his jacket, tossed it over the bannister, and she transferred her cheek to his shirt. Then he removed his tie, undid the top two buttons of his shirt, removed his cuff-links and put them in his trouser pocket, rolled back his cuffs, returned his arms to her waist. Long fingers slid up her back, touched her nape, his other hand soothed her hips, her buttocks, until she shivered, moved closer, felt the whole length of him against her, felt the slow glide of her zip, cool air against her back, and momentarily stiffened.

He soothed her, gentled her, and she relaxed again. Her mouth found his throat, slid across smooth skin as he touched her, learned her shape, and she made funny little noises of pleasure against his neck.

'Step back.'

'What?' she whispered hazily.

'Step back.'

Automatically obeying, she stared at him wide-eyed as he slipped her dress free from her shoulders, allowed it to drop to her feet, then gently brought her back against him, ran his palms over her naked shoulders and midriff, and she felt the silky material of her bra and pants slip against the material of his shirt, his trousers—a little whisper of sound that was unbelievably erotic.

'Joshua . . .' she began throatily without any very clear idea of what she wanted to say.

'Shh,' he soothed as he found her mouth with his, parted it, began to kiss her with unbelievable expertise, unhooked her bra. His palms sure and hard, he warmed her back, her ribs, halted below her breasts, thumbs extended, and she pressed closer, hiding her breasts from his touch, and he made a soft, rough sound in his throat, forced his way between their bodies until he found her erect nipples with each thumb and began to undermine what little resistance she might have had left.

Their chests might have been crushed together, but their lower bodies weren't, yet. There it was just a gentle touch, a flirtation almost, but probably far more arousing than anything more obvious. The silken barrier brushed again and again against the rougher material of his trousers, and it excited her, made her groan with desire, with frustration.

Unable to stand it any longer—the feel of his mouth, the crazy torture of his thumbs—she kicked her dress aside and pressed herself to him, sucked in a deep breath as she felt his arousal, and thought she could probably die. So long, her mind whispered—such a very long time. And passion that she had barely expressed with Andrew, had had no chance to express since he'd died, flooded through her in an overwhelming wave. As she hugged him tight, pressing closer and closer and closer, a little sob escaped her and she bit into his lip, tasted blood, wrenched her mouth free and buried it in his throat.

Hands shaking, she undid his shirt buttons, pulled the soft material free, touched her palms to his waist, his warm back, revelled in the feel of silken flesh, naked flesh against her own. She did not know how long they stood there clasped tight, not moving, barely breathing, but it seemed like for ever. So very aroused, so very unsure as to what came next, or who should instigate it, she sighed when he moved and stooped slightly, then caught her beneath her knees and carried her easily into her room, lay her on her bed—then joined her.

Leaning up on one elbow, he gently traced one finger down between her breasts, his eyes following the small movement. Then he circled each one, slowly, tantalisingly, until the pain inside, the ache, became almost overwhelming.

'Joshua,' she croaked pleadingly. Raising one hand, she slid her fingers into his hair, gripped hard, urged him closer, and he lifted his lashes, looked into her eyes, deliberately flattened out his hand, smoothed it almost roughly across her ribs, stomach, down over her pants, and stopped, a hard, heavy weight at the juncture of her thighs—and her arousal was complete. In that one moment, she would have given him anything he asked for.

He didn't ask. Still staring down at her, into her wide grey eyes, her pleading eyes, he took a deep breath, slowly released it, and with an expression on his face that she found so very hard to read he deliberately lifted his hand and rolled free. His voice thick, almost harsh, he bid her goodnight, turned

on his heel and walked out. The door was closed
very firmly behind him.

Shaken, disbelieving, a puzzled frown in her eyes,
she just lay where he had left her, stared at the door,
then shuddered. She thought that she had probably
just made a very big fool of herself. And her body
ached with lack of fulfilment. Dear God, how it
ached. The biggest insult a man could offer a
woman—and Joshua had offered it to her. Or had
he?

She heard him go into the bathroom and, a few
minutes later, his bedroom, and only then did she
move, slowly rouse herself. Feeling like a sleep-
walker, she tossed her nightie aside, found some
pyjamas—pyjamas that wouldn't have seduced an
oversexed stud—and hurried into the bathroom.

Feeling like an intruder in her own house, she
scuttled back to her room and locked the door. Not
that a lock was needed—not on her door. Joshua
probably thought he needed to lock his. And how
was she supposed to face him in the morning?
Perhaps he would leave in the night... Stop it,
Brogan! *He* started it! If he hadn't wanted...

Hurling her pillow to the floor, she dragged back
the cover and threw herself face down on the bed.
She'd coped with other things, worse things; she'd
just have to cope with this. But why? her mind
wailed. He'd been just as aroused as she'd been.

She didn't actually remember drifting into sleep,
was only aware of waking up, and found a smile
at the sight of her daughter beaming at her through
the bars of her cot.

'You look like a monkey,' she said softly, sadly, and Riffy chortled and threw her stuffed rabbit over the side. Wouldn't it be nice to be able to stay here, not have to go downstairs, meet Joshua...?

It's your house, Brogan, she told herself. And he's the one who should feel shame. Yes. So you will get up, get dressed, and go down with all flags flying. It was easy to say, but there was a hurt inside that she thought would take a very long time to heal. And she needed to know why he'd behaved like that.

The smell of frying bacon greeted her when she walked down the stairs, and, taking a deep breath for courage, clasping Riffy more firmly in her arms, she walked defiantly into the kitchen.

He turned, examined her face, and said quietly, 'If I hadn't left when I did, your expression this morning might have been even more grieved. It wasn't a rejection, Brogan; it was...' With an appealing little smile, the appeal of which Brogan fought hard against, he concluded, 'Hard. That's what it was. Grievously hard.' When she didn't answer, merely stood there, he added gently, 'I didn't want to spoil something that might be—special.'

'Then why not say so?' she demanded stiffly.

'Because it was best to go.'

Wary, wanting so very much to believe him, she queried sceptically, 'Special?'

'Yes.' Flipping over the bacon he was frying, he straightened his apron—*her* apron—and asked, 'How many eggs?'

'Eggs? I don't have eggs. I have toast.'

'This morning, dear lady, you will have egg and—'

'I'm not your dear lady,' she interrupted flatly.

'—Bacon. I did *not* walk down to the farm shop at the crack of dawn only to have my efforts rejected. Good morning, Riffy.'

Riffy blew him a raspberry. He grinned. But, watching him, Brogan got the distinct impression that the grin was—forced? No, not forced, but not as natural as yesterday. Because he was lying about his reason for leaving her yesterday? Or because it was true? But she wasn't going to lay herself open to any more of his—charm. She couldn't afford to. She should never have allowed herself to become so vulnerable. Never allowed him to get so close. And she shouldn't have drunk the wine.

'It wasn't rejection,' he insisted gently.

With a little nod, neither accepting nor believing, she fitted Riffy into her high chair and tied her bib.

'How many eggs?'

'One, thank you.'

'And Riffy? Does she eat them fried?'

'No. Scrambled, poached, boiled, but not fried.'

He nodded and, already prepared, popped an egg into a pan of boiling water, and because something—anything—needed to be said she stated quietly, 'You look very proficient.'

'Bachelors usually are. I put your battery on charge; I'll put it back in the car when I come home this evening.'

Home. 'Thank you.' Come back this evening from where? she wondered, but didn't ask.

Breakfast was a quiet meal—even Riffy behaved herself—and as soon as he was finished he stood, dropped a kiss on her hair—just like a husband, she thought sadly—kindly informed her that she could do the washing-up and left.

Seconds later, the door opened again and he put his head inside. 'It wasn't rejection,' he repeated for the second time. He watched her for a moment, nodded, and this time he did leave.

Sipping her tea, not knowing what to believe, she sighed.

Someone came to mend the cottage, mend the roof, said laconically that she didn't owe anything, that it was a favour for Joshua, and left again. The day seemed very long. It was a day of thinking, and worrying. A day of preoccupation, which was no doubt why Riffy played up, why she was fractious and wanted to be picked up all the time.

He returned at five-thirty, strolled in, smiled, touched Riffy on the head, asked if he might use the shower, and disappeared upstairs. And she wanted to kiss him, hold him, ask how his day had been, ask what happened next. He'd looked tired, grubby, hot. She poured him a chilled glass of wine—wine that she'd bought that day.

She'd fitted her battery back, driven to the nearest supermarket, returned and put the battery back on charge.

Staring at the glass, condensation blurring the sides, she nearly—nearly—poured it back in the bottle. She felt stupid, unsure. She'd cooked lasagne, and now felt embarrassed, remembered that domesticity bored him, remembered the

shudder he'd given when he'd looked at her salad—
remembered his refusal when she'd offered to cook
for him before.

He accepted the wine, even appeared grateful,
gave her a thoughtful look, smiled. He ate his
lasagne, told her it was good, then retreated to the
lounge with a book. On architecture. And all
evening she felt foolish, cross, nervous. She put
Riffy to bed, decided she couldn't cope with any
more silences, blurted out abruptly that she thought
she'd have an early night, and fled.

He ascended the stairs behind her, as swift as she,
and called softly, 'Brogan?'

She turned, waited, eyes wide, and he reproved
her, 'You didn't kiss me goodnight.'

Swallowing the lump in her throat, she made a
little sound of distress, felt her eyes fill with tears
and turned quickly away. He caught her, turned
her, pulled her into his arms and rested his chin on
her hair. 'It wasn't rejection,' he comforted her.
'We're alone in the house, and, believe me, it would
be so easy to do what I want, what you think you
want, but I think it's too soon. I think we need
more time.'

'And are you always this cautious?' she asked,
without meaning to ask that at all.

'Yes.'

'You weren't when we first met.'

He hesitated, sighed, agreed. 'No. Brogan, being
unemployed—well, it makes it difficult to make
plans...'

Instantly contrite, she hugged him, apologised.
'Joshua, I'm sorry; I never thought... It's all right;

I'm sorry for being stupid.' Feeling better, happier, she stood on tiptoe, kissed him softly on the mouth. 'I won't be pushy, I promise. Goodnight.'

She didn't see his expression, didn't wait to, just slipped into her room, stood with her back to the door. It was *pride*, she thought thankfully. Not rejection. And he had implied that she was—special, so there was time, wasn't there? Plenty of time. So why did she feel cheated? Why did she feel such a sense of dissatisfaction?

Despite her doubts, the next day was a good day, gentle and relaxing. He cut the grass for her, took them out to lunch, and *he* cooked the evening meal, and when she had put Riffy to bed she felt that little shiver of excitement at the knowledge that they would be alone for the evening.

Returning to the lounge, she stared at his back as he stood at the window staring out into the garden, and wanted to walk up behind him, hold him, talk, make plans.

'Would you like anything?' she asked quietly. 'A drink? Tea?' How domestic, she thought with inward despair, but as though he understood he turned, smiled faintly and walked towards her. 'No, but I do think we need to talk.' Resting his hands on her shoulders, he said quietly, 'I want you. You know that, don't you? *Don't* you?'

Hesitating only briefly, she nodded.

'And you want me.'

'Yes,' she whispered.

'Then you have to let him go.'

'What?'

'Daniel. You don't love him. Let go of the apron strings, Brogan.'

'Apron strings? Me?' she asked incredulously. 'All the strings are held by Daniel!'

'Not how I heard it.'

'And how did you hear it?' she demanded.

'Differently,' he said quietly. 'You aren't a fool.'

'Aren't I? I'm beginning to think I'm the biggest fool ever born. Only a fool would allow him to trample all over her the way I do. Appropriating Riffy...'

'It's understandable.'

'No, it isn't.'

'Of course it is; if you won't marry him, tell him what you intend, it's only natural he would want to be with her as much as possible.'

'Don't be absurd, and whoever gave you the idea I wanted to marry him?' And if that's what he thought, why had he been kissing her, flirting with her?

'Don't you?'

'No.'

'Then for God's sake tell him!'

'I *have*!' No, she hadn't, because she didn't believe he felt like that. 'And I don't *want* to talk about Daniel!'

'He loves you. Or thinks he does.'

'You're an authority on the subject, are you?'

'No,' he denied, sounding as tired as she felt. 'But if you don't want him, why on earth do you allow this to go on?'

'Because I don't know how to do anything else!' Her sigh deep, despairing, she walked out, stood

in the garden, stared at the dying day. And what
was he trying to say? That he wanted her but
wouldn't do anything about it because of Daniel,
because he didn't believe there was nothing between them?

'She doesn't look like him,' he commented
quietly from behind her.

'What?'

'Riffy—she doesn't look like him.'

'Look like who?' she queried, puzzled.
'Andrew?'

'No, Daniel.'

'Daniel? Why on earth would she look like
Daniel?'

He stilled, stepped up beside her, stared at her
face. 'Because he's her father?' he asked carefully.

'Her *father*?' she exclaimed in shock. '*Andrew*
is—was her father, and I find it damned insulting
of you to imply that I . . . that . . .'

'That you would sleep with Daniel immediately
after your husband's death?'

'Yes!' And if Joshua thought *that*, then why had
he wanted anything to do with her in the first place?
'Who . . . ?'

'Daniel—implied it.'

Yes, she thought with a bitter smile, but she had
hoped, assumed that no one actually believed it.
'Makes me out to be a really nice person, doesn't
it? What else did he *imply*?'

'That because he was now crippled you were
hesitating about marrying him.'

'*What?*' More hurt than she would have believed possible, even though she had suspected some of it, she turned her face away to hide her distress.

'Tell me,' he said, and his voice was insistent, urgent almost, and that didn't make any sort of sense. If he knew all this, thought all this, what difference did it make now? Would he forgive her? Kiss her? Fall in love with her?

'Tell me,' he repeated.

'No. It isn't any of your business.' And talking about it to a stranger—stranger, she thought almost hysterically, when she'd practically invited him into her bed?—smacked of disloyalty. Although if Daniel was going round telling such lies, or implying them anyway, she didn't exactly owe him any loyalty, did she?

Joshua stepped in front of her, searched her averted face. 'You look—betrayed,' he said quietly.

'I feel betrayed. And not only by Daniel.'

'Brogan—'

'Don't,' she said fiercely. 'And if you thought Riffy was Daniel's daughter, thought I was going to marry him, why the *hell* did you pursue me? Because I will *not* believe that you saw me and fell instantly in love!'

'No,' he agreed. 'Not love. Attraction. And I didn't, then, know about Daniel. Now tell me why you feel betrayed by him.'

'Because he told everyone the accident was my fault,' she burst out, 'that I was speeding, and I wasn't. I feel guilty and ashamed, but I wasn't speeding. And there *was* a motorbike,' she added earnestly.

'And he trades on your guilt?'

'Yes.' And suddenly finding a need to say it, all of it, she cried, 'He's got it into his head that I *owe* him, and I *do*, but not with my freedom, not my life! He's persuaded himself that there's more between us than there is, that he has a *right* to Riffy, to me. I don't *mind* the cooking and the cleaning, the helping, because I *did* put him in the wheelchair, and I'll feel guilty for the rest of my life! But how long do I have to go on *paying*? He needs other friends, a life of his own, and I can't...'

Taking a deep breath, distressed and close to tears, she walked away, stood at the edge of the field, stared blindly ahead, was aware of him following, wished passionately that she had said nothing, but as though those few words had burst the dam she continued almost to herself, 'He was there for me when Andrew died, as a friend. He was unbelievably kind, thoughtful. He was there when Riffy was born, but he isn't her father, he isn't my lover, he's just a—friend. And I don't know what to do any more,' she added listlessly. 'I don't even know how badly he's injured.'

'Psychologically,' he said quietly.

Swinging round, shocked, she demanded, 'What?'

'The doctors don't think there's permanent damage; they think it's mostly in his mind. But he refused counselling, and no one can make him have it. It has to be his own decision.'

'You mean he could walk if he *wanted* to?' If he'd been pretending all this time, trading on her guilt...

'So I believe.' He continued to observe her, *carefully* observe her, then glanced at his watch and added, 'I don't mean that he's pretending; I think he genuinely believes he's crippled. But it's in the mind, not the body.'

'So he could be cured,' she said quietly.

'Yes,' he agreed cautiously—a caution she didn't notice.

Staring at him, examining his face, she asked quietly, 'How do you know all this?'

'I made it my business to find out. If there was a chance of him walking again, of your responsibility ending, then I needed to know—know how much of a chance there was for me.'

'For you?'

'Yes.'

'There was always a chance, Joshua,' she said softly.

'So it does make a difference?'

'Of *course* it makes a difference! All the difference in the world.' Her mind racing, considering all the implications, the possibilities, she murmured thoughtfully, 'And in two years—less now—he'll come into his inheritance...'

'Will he?' he asked quietly.

'Yes. The money was left in trust until he's thirty.' Still following her own line of thought, not noticing Joshua's stillness, she murmured, 'And two years isn't so long, is it?'

Although, maybe it would be better for his character if he could make good before that time, become famous, she thought with a sad smile. Poor Daniel so desperately yearned to be famous. But he would never do anything all the time he stayed here, would he? Being brutal now might make him sit up and take notice. Anger might be the spur he needed to cure his apathy. It might even cure her own. And if his injuries *were* psychological...

A look of determination, resolution on her face, and as though he could possibly know what she was talking about, she added defiantly, 'We deserve it, Riffy and me. I know what to do, as soon as he comes back—'

'Deserve what? Payment for services rendered? A life of ease?'

Still absent, still thinking, she nodded. 'Something like that, yes.'

'And what about us?' Joshua asked quietly.

'Us?' she echoed.

'Yes.'

Staring at him, she looked bewildered for a moment, because their feelings for each other would in no way be affected by what happened to Daniel, would they? 'I don't understand.'

'Don't you?'

'No.' Searching his eyes, she said quietly, 'It won't make any difference to us. How can it?'

'You want it to continue?'

Feeling suddenly frightened, she whispered, 'Yes. Don't you? You said...'

'It wasn't rejection.'

'Yes. It wasn't, was it?'

He hesitated, and his smile seemed bitter. 'No,' he denied quietly.

'Then how will it affect us? You think he will mind? Is that it? Well, I expect he will at first, but I can't allow him to run my life, Joshua. Not any more.'

'No.'

'And don't you think it's best that he understands that now?'

'Oh, yes, I definitely think it's best that he understands.' Reaching for her, he pulled her close, and his expertise, his experience sent all other thoughts, concerns skidding. With a mumbled cry, she slid her arms round his neck, welcomed back the warmth, the promise.

'Is that why you've been so—contrary? Because you thought I was involved with Daniel?'

'Mmm.'

'And now that you know I'm not?'

'What do you think?' He undid her shirt, found that she wore no bra, slid his hand inside, undid his own shirt, and pressed her close until she groaned, wanting more. She urgently rubbed her breasts against his naked chest, felt the cool evening air caress her, arched her neck, invited his touch. 'Oh, Joshua. Let's go inside.'

'No.' His voice sounded strained—unbelievably strained—as he bent, captured a swollen nipple between his teeth. 'I want to take you here, on the ground, in the open, beneath the sky...'

'No,' she said thickly, 'not here; please not here.'

'Why? There's no one to see.'

'Someone might come.' Embarrassed, her breathing laboured, not used to such uninhibited behaviour, fingernails digging into his shoulders, she tried to push him away, but the sensations rioting through her body made her weak. The feel of his mouth on her breast made her weak.

He wrenched her shirt aside, ignored her cry of distress, and, his hands gripping her elbows, he pulled her up onto her toes—just as Amanda's van hurtled round the corner and screeched to a halt beside them.

CHAPTER SIX

'No-o-o,' Daniel yelled. He flung open his door, tried to clamber out, fell, and Joshua released her, went to get his wheelchair and help him into it.

Daniel wrenched himself free. 'Don't touch me,' he ordered viciously. 'I *trusted* you! And *you*,' he shouted at Brogan as she fumbled to do up her shirt. 'How *could* you? Don't you know who he *is*?'

'Daniel—' Joshua began, his voice cool and controlled.

'Shut up! You think I don't *know*? I've spoken to my mother, you fool! And my mother, as you should know—because you do know my mother, don't you?—is quite incapable of keeping anything secret!' Swinging back to Brogan, his face bitter and distorted, he raged, 'He's a *spy*! Sent by my parents to make a little gold-digger let go of their son!'

'Gold-digger?' Brogan whispered in bewilderment. '*Gold*-digger?'

'Yes! He knew what time I'd be back. He was in collusion with Amanda, but she couldn't go through with it. *Told* me! A set-up!' he yelled. 'Make sure I saw you. A trade-off! He thought you'd go for his wealth instead of mine! Expected me to come back and be surprised, hurt!'

'He doesn't have any wealth,' Brogan contradicted him blankly.

'Yes, he does! He thought I would pack up, leave, realise what a fool I'd been! Well, I was certainly a fool for believing he was no threat! Certainly a fool for believing he wouldn't go out of his way to show you how a *real* man could perform,' he sneered. '*He* wasn't crippled, was he? He could make love to you properly! I *loved* you!' he yelled. 'I've *always* loved you!'

'No...'

'Yes! You think *he* wants you?' he laughed bitterly. 'You think he was kissing you because he *cared*? Because you turned him on? Well, go on, ask him,' he urged.

Feeling sick, faint, shaky, she glanced at Joshua—a still, carved Joshua, who stared back at her with cold, dark eyes.

'He wasn't broke!' Daniel continued viciously. 'He was bored!'

'But did need to be in Suffolk,' Joshua drawled mildly.

'Yes, it added zest to the game,' Daniel spat bitterly. 'You like games, don't you, Joshua? Like women. He has a whole string of them!' he shouted at Brogan. 'You really think he wanted *you*? Oh, you're pretty enough, sexy enough, but he likes his freedom, does Josh. Love 'em and leave 'em— that's his motto. And you think he wanted a *baby* cluttering up his love life?'

His words tumbling over themselves, vitriol spilling forth as though it had been dammed up for weeks, months, he wheeled himself up to Brogan, bumped her knees hard enough to hurt. 'Sleepless nights? Food dribbled on his expensive suits? I would have given *anything*—anything,' he choked, 'for you and Riffy. I was giving you *time*! Didn't want to rush you!' With a twisted laugh, he derided her, 'What were you, in bed before I was even out of sight?'

'No,' she denied thickly. Staring once more at Joshua, not angry, just sick, she asked quietly, 'Is this true?'

He didn't answer, just continued to watch her.

'But I told you the truth.'

'You also told me that you knew what to do, that you and Riffy deserved something.'

'Peace,' she explained, still quiet. 'He owed me peace.'

'You talked about his wealth.'

'Because if his injuries were psychological then insisting he go might have snapped him out of it, whereas his staying here wouldn't have done. And the reason I needed to know he had money was so that I could be sure that if he didn't make it as a designer he would at least have money to fall back on. I couldn't have let him go just to see him rough it, not have enough to eat, because I knew he wouldn't apply to his parents.'

'Rough it?' Daniel snarled. 'Peace? You wrecked my life!'

'Yes,' she agreed, 'but that doesn't mean you can live mine. Whatever I did, it doesn't give you the right to make my choices for me. You allowed people to think Riffy was yours, told Joshua—and how many others?—that I wouldn't marry you because you were crippled. Didn't you?'

'I *loved* you!'

'And that makes it all right? Nothing will change what I did. Nothing will take away the guilt. But this is my life, Daniel, and Riffy is my daughter. I'm fond of you, grateful to you—'

'I don't want your gratitude!'

'But I have nothing else,' she said gently, hurting for him, for herself, shaking so badly inside, feeling so sick, but somehow determined that Joshua would never know it.

She continued, 'I never gave you reason to believe that I would ever marry you, did I? That I would ever come to love you? You persuaded yourself that it would happen, because you wanted it to, and I was partly at fault because I didn't know how to tell you, make it plainer without being brutal. After all you had done for me, I thought I owed you peace of mind, thought you would wake up one day, realise what you were doing, what you were missing, that there was a whole life out there waiting to be lived. After your fashion show, I told myself. When you had a job—'

'But I love you,' he repeated.

'No...'

'Yes! Don't tell me how I feel! Don't you *dare*! I've always loved you. Before Andrew died, I loved you. I didn't expect you to love me back at once. I was prepared to wait ... I looked after you, after the baby. It was *me* who held her, bathed her, fed her. It was me who looked after you.'

'I know, but—'

'And then *he* came, and you *lied* to me. You don't even know who he is, do you? Joshua Baynard Renwick,' he mocked bitterly. 'One of our most gifted architects. A fervent campaigner for historical restoration. An expert. When I found out what my parents had done, I looked him up. He's really quite famous, wealthy. And a friend of my father! My father's little lackey, sent to keep an eye on me! Get me out of the clutches of a mercenary little widow. And do you know what else my dear parents thought? That you were living in *my* house.'

Joshua made a small, involuntary movement and Daniel swung back to him and sneered, 'Didn't know that, did you? You thought it was my house, that she'd dumped herself on me, was pretending to care, living here rent-free... Fools, all of you! Didn't my sainted parents give me credit for *anything*? Did they think me *stupid*? I loved her!'

Dragging in a deep, shuddery breath, on the edge of tears, he continued bitterly, 'And so he joined your tour group, pretended an interest, and you, you stupid little fool, fell for it. He made you rent him the cottage, and it was all a *lie*! He came to lure you, away from me, and when he'd succeeded, when I'd left, when he'd shown me what you were *really* like, he would have dumped you—smiled his nasty smile, and dumped you!'

His face was so anguished, so hurting that she wanted to hold him, comfort him, and she knew that she mustn't.

'If it hadn't been for that motorbi—' Breaking off, realising what he'd said, he thumped his fist on the arm of his chair in bitter frustration.

'So you did see it,' she whispered. 'Oh, Daniel. Why? All this time...' Eyes bleak, she stared first at Daniel then at Joshua. 'And how far would you have gone,' she asked him, 'in your pursuit of truth? All the way? Such a sacrifice for you. Such a bloody sacrifice.'

Her voice breaking, she took a moment to compose herself, then said quietly and with great dignity, 'Now please leave. Both of you.' Throat blocked, eyes burning, she walked inside and up to her room. Closing the door, she locked it—the second time she had ever done so, the second time she had ever been glad that it did so.

Learn your lessons the hard way, don't you, Brogan? Tears streaming down her face, a hard, painful lump in her chest, she lay on the bed, hugged the pillow tight. She felt used, and cheap, and so unbelievably betrayed.

She could hear them talking through the open window, Daniel bitter, Joshua quiet. And then, moments later, the handle rattled, a knock sounded. She ignored it.

'Brogan,' Joshua called quietly.

She ignored him, held her breath, listened to the silence—the silence of someone waiting.

She heard, or thought she heard, a sigh, heard his footsteps retreat, heard his car start up a few minutes later. Heard the van. And only then did she move. Rolling onto her back, she stared up at the ceiling. Unbelievably, it was still light.

You must have known, Brogan. In your heart of hearts you must have known it wasn't right. The clues had all been there... Hated domesticity—he'd *said* that. He'd blown hot and blown cold. There'd been the sudden helpfulness when before he'd been cold, unemotional. But you were lonely and vul-

nerable, wanted to believe, and so, with the first
attractive man to come into your orbit, you hung
your common sense in the wardrobe and made it
easy for him. He excited you, made you feel like a
woman again... Gullible.

Tears filled her eyes, overflowed. Never again
would she scoff at little newspaper articles about
women being duped. Fools, she'd always said, could
they not see? How vulnerable had those women
been? Had they too looked into a future that
seemed bleak, without romance?

Not a nice man, Joshua Baynard. No, even that
was a lie. Joshua Baynard *Renwick*. She could have
accepted him keeping an eye on Daniel.
Understood. But to deliberately set out to attract
her? Even if he had thought her a gold-digger...
No, that hadn't been nice, and it cheapened him,
not her.

Stirring, realising that the shadows were length-
ening, that soon it would be dark, and not even
bothering to wipe away her tears, she walked
downstairs to lock up.

Joshua was sitting in the kitchen. Waiting.

She stared at him, felt nothing.

'What would you have done, I wonder, if I hadn't
been attracted to you?'

'That wasn't originally the plan.'

'Which was?'

'Won't you sit down?' he invited her quietly.

'No.'

He nodded, accepting, his face as empty as it ever
had been. 'Originally, just as Daniel said, the in-

tention was to see what was going on, ensure Daniel was all right, keep an eye on him.'

'But you needed an entry, a reason for being here, and when you saw how you affected me you changed the rules.'

'To my shame, yes. If you were the sort of person that Daniel's parents had portrayed you to be, thought you to be—'

'Giving me a taste of my own medicine was no more than I deserved?'

'Yes.'

'Then I would very much like to know how—if, as Daniel's father supposedly implied, I would not marry him because he was crippled—I could also be a gold-digger. Surely one cancels out the other?'

'No,' he disagreed, still quiet, still—sincere, damn him. 'It was assumed you were holding out for a bigger slice.'

'Assumed?' she echoed softly.

'Yes—assumed that a settlement was in the offing.'

'But it wasn't.'

'No.'

'You weren't unemployed?'

His hesitation was brief. 'No.'

'You deliberately played on my sympathy, in fact.'

The hesitation was even briefer before he nodded. 'Yes.'

'And just out of curiosity,' she asked, her face uncharacteristically hard, 'how far would you have taken it?'

'I wouldn't have taken it anywhere, or not for those reasons. I was falling in love with you, Brogan...'

'Love!' she scoffed bitterly.

'Yes, *love*. I was already backing off, wanting to know you—the real you—and if you hadn't said what you did out by the field... If I hadn't misunderstood...'

'Oh, you do agree that you misunderstood?'

'Yes.'

'It *was* a set-up, then?'

He hesitated again, then nodded, eyes still on hers. 'Yes. I arrogantly decided that Amanda would be a better—companion for him, and so I went to see her, explained about Daniel's parents, about how worried they were that you were a bad influence on him—even,' he added with a slightly bitter smile, 'that you were impeding his recovery. Naturally, she was horrified, and agreed to help me. We decided that if he saw you kissing me—'

'Oh, not only kissing,' she said derisively, 'but half-naked...'

He looked down, gave a gentle sigh, which Brogan chose not to believe was ashamed, he agreed quietly, 'Yes, but when Amanda had thought it over, remembered that she'd liked you, she told Daniel the plan. We'd arranged a time for her to arrive—'

'And the rest, as they say, is history.'

'Yes. And I'm not to be forgiven for misjudging you, am I?'

'No. Neither are you to be forgiven for—' Breaking off, she gave a small, bitter laugh. For giving me hope, she silently completed—for giving me joy.

Hurting, her voice husky, she ordered quietly, 'Go away, Joshua. Right away. Don't ever come back.' Turning on her heel, she walked up to her room and locked herself in. All the whys and wherefores in the world would make no difference, would they? No. Only one fact remained: Joshua Baynard had made a fool of her. Deliberately.

CHAPTER SEVEN

BROGAN woke in the morning feeling listless and stupid and betrayed, but as she stared at her wan face in the mirror her apathy turned to anger. There had been no apology, no 'I'm sorry Brogan, for being so mistaken in you', just a quiet question about whether he was to be forgiven.

Had he shrugged an indifferent shoulder, driven off to pastures new? Or was the pasture old—a resident girlfriend somewhere? 'Darling,' she would exclaim, 'how perfectly dreadful for you! Forced to kiss her?' Would she shudder delicately, take him to her bed to help him forget?

He'd said he'd been falling in love with her. No. If he'd been falling in love, he would have told her, explained.

Not a nice man, Brogan. No. So why did it hurt so much? Why couldn't she *hate* him? She *wanted* to! Wrenching her mind away, she picked up her gurgling daughter, hugged her tight, went to get them both ready for a day that held no promises.

By next week you'll have forgotten it, she assured herself. Be able to laugh about it. Will revel in your new-found peace.

Entering the kitchen, she came to a shocked halt. A large—very large—bouquet of flowers rested there. Cellophane, pink ribbon, an envelope, and a note.

159

Mouth tight, she snatched it up, unfolded it.

'"I've moved back into the cottage,"' she read. '"Enclosed is this week's rent."' It was signed, 'J.B.R.'

Without thought, face set, Riffy under one arm, flowers under the other, note and envelope scrunched in her hand, she stormed across to the cottage, slammed open the door—and found him waiting, wearing only a towel.

'Isn't this where we came in?' he queried softly, but his eyes were still, quiet, watching.

She threw the envelope and note at him, then the flowers, and stormed out. Riffy protested. Loudly.

'Be quiet,' Brogan said softly, crossly. 'You have no judgement.' And how dared he? How *dared* he?

Back in the kitchen, plonking Riffy in her high chair, she slammed the kettle on, shoved bread in the toaster, mashed a Weetabix for her daughter, crushed it, ground it, stabbed it, then hurled the spoon across the kitchen. How *dared* he?

Striding back and forth, castigating him, herself, she slammed her hand onto the table—and saw Joshua watching her through the open back door. Striding across, she hit him.

'I *hate* you!'

'Yes,' he said quietly.

'Go away.'

He searched her poor unhappy face, glanced at Riffy, who was looking absolutely riveted, and walked out. He was still wearing the towel.

'I hate you,' she whispered. Closing the back door, she forced herself to be calm. She fed Riffy, drank a cup of tea, tidied up, then went shopping.

She remembered halfway to the shops that she hadn't replaced the battery, which meant that *he* must have done so, and was tempted to turn round, take it out and leave it on his doorstep. Then she realised how stupid she was being—and anyway, it wasn't *his* doorstep, it was hers, because the cottage belonged to her. And how could he move back? The bed was still in Riffy's nursery. Perhaps he was intending to put it back whilst she was gone; perhaps he was going to sleep on the floor.

She couldn't remember what she wanted from the supermarket, came out with hardly anything, and when she arrived back his car was gone, the cottage locked, windows closed tight. And she felt—cheated.

Opening the back door, Riffy under one arm, shopping clutched awkwardly to her chest, she halted in disbelief. The flowers she had thrown at him were arranged in a vase on the table; there were more flowers in the hall, the lounge, the landing, and there was a little bunch of violets in the bathroom. It was too late for violets. Violets came out in the spring. Bewildered, miserable, tired, she made Riffy's lunch.

If he'd been there, she assured herself, she would have gathered them all up and thrown them at him. But he wasn't. He'd gone.

At six she heard a car. Stilling, eyes wide, she ran to lock the back door. Yanking down the blind, she leaned against the door, listened. She heard a car door slam, heard the cottage door open, heard it close, and cautiously peeped out.

A gleaming Mercedes stood proudly in the lane, and, as she watched, the cottage windows were flung wide. Seconds later he emerged, and she hastily dropped the blind back into place, put her back flat to the door. Riffy watched with interest. Brogan gave her a lame smile.

She heard footsteps, heard them stop, then retreat.

Peeping carefully out, she saw an enormous arrangement of roses in a wicker basket on the step.

Yanking on the door, she remembered she'd locked it, so she flung the window open and yelled, 'Don't keep bringing me flowers!'

He turned, asked interestedly, 'Are we talking?'

'No!' She slammed the window shut, and Riffy shrieked with delight.

'Be quiet, you,' Brogan reproved her. 'It's not funny.'

Riffy screwed up her face, scrunched up her eyes, and burbled something totally incomprehensible.

The next morning it was fruit, alongside the wilting roses. Apples, pears, grapes, oranges, bananas—every conceivable fruit available, imaginable. She liked fruit... Slamming the door on temptation, she left them there. It's an awful waste, Brogan... I don't care, she argued with herself.

In the evening it was perfume, the next morning glossy magazines, then—nothing.

'Cheapskate,' she muttered. Disappointed, she retreated indoors, unaware that she was watched from the cottage.

The next morning, there was still nothing, and
he didn't go to work—if he had work. Perhaps even
that had been a lie. Maybe there was no Norman
keep. The car had been a lie, why not the keep?
And the cottage remained closed, windows shut.

By twelve, not even admitting to herself that she
was on constant watch, that she had washing to put
out, rubbish to empty, she got their lunch, washed
up. 'Oh-h-h, this is ridiculous,' she said at last.
Grabbing her laundry basket, she marched outside,
closely followed by Riffy pushing the elephant, and
defiantly hung out her washing.

Nothing.

Beginning to be alarmed, she stared at the silent
cottage. Was he ill? He must be *stifling* in there
with the doors and windows shut. And she was
halfway to the cottage before she'd even realised
what she was doing. Quickly checking that Riffy
wasn't up to mischief, wasn't eating mud or anything that was even more unsavoury, she peered in
the bedroom window. Joshua was lying face down
in a camp-bed, unmoving.

Dithering, she tapped, then tapped harder.
Nothing. Chewing her lip, checking Riffy again, she
walked round to the front of the cottage, tried the
door. It was unlocked.

'Joshua?' she called.

Silence.

She tutted. Marching back to her daughter who,
elephant abandoned, was playing with the peg-bag,
she picked her up, bag and all, marched back and
into the cottage, shoved open the bedroom door
and marched in.

'Joshua!' He didn't move—made no sign at all that he had heard. 'Joshua?' she whispered worriedly. Creeping over to the bed, she hesitantly reached out to touch his shoulder, then yelped in fright when a hand shot out, grabbed her wrist and tugged.

'You—'

'Uh—uh, remember small ears,' he cautioned her.

'I thought you were *ill*!' she retorted furiously.

'It's a wonder I'm not dead,' he returned mildly. 'I'm probably severely dehydrated. Took your time, didn't you?' Tousled and sweaty, he watched her, refusing to release her wrist.

Tumbled across him, Riffy still clutched awkwardly, she struggled. 'You're hurting me.'

'No, I'm not.' He dragged her closer, kissed her. 'Good morning.'

'It's afternoon! And you're sweaty!'

'I'll have a shower in a minute. Going to join me?'

'No!'

'Coward.'

'Let go of me!'

'No. Hello, Riffy.'

Riffy beamed, grabbed his hair, lurched out from Brogan's hold and scrambled under the covers. Joshua laughed, wriggled, yelped, and groped for her with his other hand. Peering under the bedclothes, he snorted, quickly moved away from searching fingers, widened his eyes in shock and hastily rolled free, dragging Brogan with him.

'You don't have anything on!' she protested in horror, and quickly shut her eyes.

'Of course I don't!' he exclaimed, his laughter smothered. 'Why else would I be trying to avoid your daughter's groping fingers?'

Unaware that he watched her, that his eyes held a sadness, a prayer, that he looked—loving, she felt movement, heard her daughter gurgle with laughter, half opened one eye, saw that Joshua was trying to fend Riffy off one-handed, and quickly closed it again.

'Put something on!'

'Can't—haven't got a free hand.'

Riffy was clasped firmly, Brogan tugged upright then pulled into the miniscule bathroom—and into the shower.

'No!' she yelped as water drenched her. Opening her eyes, she glared at an equally wet Joshua and a delighted Riffy who was holding her face up to the spray, mouth open. The child choked, coughed, and spat. Brogan snapped the water off.

'If I let go,' he said quietly, 'will you stay? Please?'

She looked down, became aware of where she was actually looking, jerked her head up again, flushed.

'Please?' he repeated.

'You spent all that money and it was *wasted*! Flowers dying, fruit going soft...'

'Not wasted.'

'It was stupid! I told you to go!'

'I didn't want to go. Please?'

'You cheated.'

'Not entirely,' he denied.

'Don't lie. You pretended.'

'Only at first. I *was* attracted to you, Brogan.'

'And that makes it all right?' she asked bitterly.

'No, and the more I got to know you, the less all right it became.'

'Not rejection,' she said with a bitter laugh.

'Neither was it, but I . . .'

'Couldn't make love to a woman you thought a cheat, a liar and a gold-digger, could you? My, my, how you must have hated yourself even being *aroused* by me!'

'Stop it,' he said quietly. 'I understand your bitterness; I understand your pain—'

'Do you? Do you really? You *hurt* me!'

'I know.'

'Didn't even apologise.'

'I know.'

'You *used* me!'

'No—'

'Yes!' she argued fiercely.

'But that isn't why you're angry, is it?' he asked gently. 'It's because you think I made a fool of you.'

'You did!'

'No,' he denied. 'I made a fool of myself. I behaved in a way that was not only reprehensible but contrary to any ethical code I've ever believed in. Will you allow me to explain *why* I did what I did?'

Moving her head in a distressed little gesture that was neither negative nor affirmative, she pushed her sopping hair off her face with one hand, the other still in Joshua's grasp. 'Why? Because you want my forgiveness?' she asked with a bitterness that she couldn't quite hide.

'I do want your forgiveness—of course I do. But that isn't the only reason.'

'Then what else is there? What do you want from me?'

'All you have to give,' he said simply.

'What?'

'Give me your promise not to run away, and I'll release you.'

She finally nodded. It was a little cautious, but it was an agreement nevertheless.

He held her eyes for a moment longer, released her, handed Riffy to her together with the sopping peg-bag, and ordered gently, 'Go and get out of those wet things. I'll meet you on neutral ground. Middle of the lawn? In ten minutes?'

With another nod, all the fire gone out of her, she trailed out and across to the cottage. She changed them both, put Riffy out in her pram to have a sleep, walked listlessly across to the old apple tree, stood beneath its welcoming shade.

Leaning against the trunk, absently picking at the bark with agitated fingers, she stared out across the fields. And if you listen to any more of his lies, Brogan, allow him to—beguile you all over again, then you're a fool, she told herself. You're already halfway to believing whatever he might be going to say.

She heard him come out, moved her gaze downwards, saw his feet come into her line of vision.

'I cannot *bear*,' he began quietly, 'to see you looking so hurt and unhappy. I cannot *bear* the knowledge that I caused it. We all betrayed you, didn't we—Daniel's parents, Daniel, me? Even your husband, by dying so young, betrayed you.'

Reaching out, he took her hand, held it loosely in his. 'Daniel's father is a builder. A good builder, a craftsman. He's also an historian, and a few years ago when I needed someone to help restore an ancient barn. Daniel's father applied. We became good friends. He's bluff, blunt and unimpeachably honest. A man's man if you like, and Daniel, the only child he had—could have—was the apple of his eye.

'When I first met you, I'd just come from Prague; I'd been working out there for months, along with Daniel's father. There's an awful lot of restoration work that needs doing and not enough experts. Restoration is something we both passionately believe in. Anyway, he told me about Daniel's accident, about you... He was angry, confused, bitter. Daniel wouldn't talk to him, had virtually cut himself off from his mother, who yearned to look after him, and he said, "She looks so bloody innocent, all big eyes and long legs." He knew your husband,' Joshua added quietly.

Glancing up, she gave him a puzzled look. He'd said it almost significantly. 'Yes, I imagine he did,' she agreed. 'Andrew and Daniel went to school together. Andrew even worked for him for a while, I believe.'

'Yes. He wanted Andrew to stay working for him.'

'Did he? I didn't know that. But what has this to do with—?'

'Andrew apparently said, when he left, that the reason he could no longer work for him was that the girl he'd just met, the girl he'd fallen in love with wouldn't marry someone who worked for someone else. That she wanted them to have their own business.'

'Oh, that's not true,' she whispered. 'He *can't* have said that.'

'Daniel's father said he did, and I believe him, but maybe it was said as an excuse, to make the leaving easier. I didn't know your husband, didn't know what he was like.'

But she did, and it did sound like something he might have said. Andrew had always liked things to be easy, wanted people to like him, not blame him, and so perhaps he *had* blamed his leaving on her. It hadn't been likely that she would ever meet Daniel's father, and certainly no one would ever have envisaged circumstances like these. 'And so he thought me mercenary,' she murmured. 'And in the light of recent events...'

'Believed it utterly,' he agreed. 'He also gave Daniel some money, quite a lot of money—his college fees and enough to buy a small apartment. And so when Daniel wrote to his mother from here—'

'They thought this was his house.'

'Yes. It doesn't seem to have occurred to them to ask why he would buy a house in Suffolk when his college was in London, but that's what they thought, and that you and Andrew had moved in.'

'I see.'

'They also thought...' With a little sigh, a slight hesitation, he continued, 'They also thought that you and Daniel were lovers, that you were cheating on your husband. Daniel's infrequent letters were full of you—how lovely you were, how much he admired you. Maybe he didn't realise how much he mentioned your name, how misleading he was being—I don't know—but when Andrew died, when Daniel told them he was looking after you, and when the baby came implied more or less that she was his, they were at first angry, then accepting, sensible enough to know that if they alienated you they would never see their grandchild...'

With a distressed little sound, she wrenched her hand free, turned her back. Oh, dear God.

'They wanted desperately to come down, meet you, see the baby. Daniel said you refused to do so.'

'And then came the accident,' she said quietly. 'An accident I caused. So not only had I cheated on my husband, robbed them of their grandchild, but I had now crippled their only son. But he was so infatuated with me,' she added bitterly, 'that he insisted I stay here, have the run of the house—*his* house—whilst he was forced to live in the annexe. And not only *that*, but I was also hanging out for a slice of his inheritance.'

'Yes.'

'What a nasty little person I must have seemed. And all based on speculation, assumption... Why on earth didn't they come to see what sort of person I was for themselves?'

'They did. You were out, and Daniel told them never to come here again.'

'Because if they did, and met me, found out the truth—'

'Daniel's chance of having you fall in love with him was gone. He seems to have thought that if he loved you long enough, stayed constant long enough—'

'Blackmailed me long enough, played on my guilt long enough...'

'Yes, and so, when his father told me all this in Prague, was so very worried—no, anguished—and when he learned I had to be in Norfolk—'

'Norfolk?' she swung round to exclaim.

He gave a wry smile. 'Yes, Norfolk. That's where the Norman keep is.'

'But Norfolk's miles away! The next county!'

'I know. Believe me, I know. Driving back and forth in this heat, in that old car...'

'But why? Why the pretence of being poor?'

'Because you assumed I was. I'd come straight from the airport, hadn't had time to even shower and change before my flight; the only car I could rent was—highly unsatisfactory,' he murmured wryly.

'And not at all what you were used to,' she put in somewhat pithily.

'No. I was hot, tired, irritable. I stopped in Lavenham, enquired at the information office for directions to here—and saw a poster advertising a tour of the village for that day—that afternoon—and the name of the tour guide was crossed out and your name written in above it. Simple. So unbelievably simple.'

'Chrissie was sick,' she explained unnecessarily. 'She's a friend of mine. I was filling in. Just for that one week. Her mum looked after Riffy whilst I did it.'

'I expected to meet an older woman, someone hard, aggressive, and saw, as Daniel's father had done, all big eyes and long legs. A friendly smile. But I *believed* all he had said. I had no reason not to. *He* believed it. And my mother married my father for money,' he tacked on softly. 'I saw firsthand what it can do. I thought Daniel deserved better. *Everyone* deserves better than what my father put up with. But he loved my mother. He put up with all her bitching, her affairs, her coldness, because he loved her. I don't think he was ever even sure that I was his son. But he behaved as though I was, and I loved him for that.'

'And so, when Daniel's father asked...'

'Yes. I didn't want to come, didn't think it was any of my business, thought Daniel was old enough to do as he liked. He wasn't a child, and I had no reason to suppose he was a fool. Had no reason to suppose he was manipulative. And you were the least likely looking gold-digger I have ever seen. But looks can be deceptive. My *mother* had been deceptive. All I ever intended then was to find out the facts, report back and go home. But you intrigued me, and so I stayed.

'When we went out to dinner, Mario said, "This one we like, Joshua," and I no longer wanted to pretend with something that felt so good. So in a way that night my behaviour *was* rejection—a rejection of my feelings for you. Feelings I didn't want. And even if you'd turned out to be a gold-digger I would still have wanted you. As did my father my mother. Ironic, I thought. History repeating itself.'

'You could have told me,' she murmured. 'I would have understood.'

'Yes, but I didn't know that.'

'No.'

'Did you love him so very much, Brogan?'

'Andrew?' And when he nodded she hesitated for a moment, before explaining, 'I did love him, but it wasn't quite as I'd hoped, imagined. If he hadn't died, I imagine we would have had a good marriage. Perhaps not exciting, or breathless, but a solid marriage. He tended to be a bit single-minded, not very intuitive... I wasn't unhappy, just...'

'Just not very fulfilled? No, don't answer that if it feels disloyal. All I was trying to discover—'

'Was why I reacted to you like a bitch on heat?'

'No! Brogan, no. You can't think I thought that!'

'Can't I? Thank you for explaining,' she added quietly.

Face impassive, he waited, then finally asked, 'That's it?'

Eyes lowered, she nodded. 'Yes.'

'No forgiveness?'

She hesitated, an awful lump in her throat, a sick pain in her stomach. 'I forgive you,' she murmured huskily.

'But?'

Taking a deep breath, ragged and uneven, she said, 'But I don't want to see you again.'

'Because?'

'Because I've been hurt enough.'

CHAPTER EIGHT

JOSHUA stared at her for a long time, dark eyes unfathomable, and then he asked quietly, 'You expect that I will hurt you more?'

'I don't know. You have the—capability.'

'And the risk isn't worth taking?'

'I have Riffy; I can't afford risk.' She was going to cry, she knew she was, could feel her lower lip begin to tremble. 'Please go,' she whispered. 'If you care for me at all, please go.'

He reached out, touched her mouth with one finger. 'For now,' he agreed softly. Turning, he walked quickly away, climbed into his car, and drove away. She didn't watch him go. He no longer wore jeans and a faded shirt, no longer had the need to pretend. His dark trousers had looked expensive, as had his shirt. His car certainly was. Had his mother loved him?

Blinking back useless tears, she walked inside, stared at the flowers he had sent. Perhaps she would move, put the house up for sale, start afresh somewhere else. A new life. And perhaps, one day, she'd find someone to love. Someone else.

Days passed, but he didn't go away, not from her mind, her heart. She wasn't sleeping properly, wasn't eating properly, and that wasn't fair to Riffy.

It felt like being bereaved all over again. She cleared out the cottage, lingered over the things he had left, the things he had touched. The drawing-board was gone, and his briefcase. She sat on the bed he had left, and felt a poor little fool. Every time a car went past on the road, she would become still, listen hard, then sigh when it went past. And then, exactly two weeks after he had left, Daniel came. A quiet, chastened Daniel, driven by Amanda.

Riffy shrieked with delight, scrambled onto his lap, and he held her tight, kissed her silky hair.

'I missed her,' he said huskily. 'Missed you both.'

'Daniel—'

'No, let me say it. I need to apologise, explain, if I can.' Riffy cuddled in his arms, he stared at her and said quietly, 'You look terrible. We did that to you, didn't we?'

'Yes.'

'I've spoken to my parents, explained,' he hurried on quickly. 'They were horrified, angry... They'd like to meet you, apologise—'

'Not yet,' she interrupted quickly. 'One day...'

'Yes. Oh, Brogan, I don't even know where to begin. I always envied him, you know—Andrew. He got the best grades in school, the best girls... Perhaps that was part of it. I was so used to wanting what he had... You were so pretty and funny, always smiling... I'm so sorry. I've made your life hell, and that was never my intention. I didn't pretend to be crippled...'

'I know.'

'I tried to stand in Andrew's shoes, make them fit. Make them fit better,' he added awkwardly. 'You'd look so hurt sometimes, sad, when he overrode your ideas, your enthusiasm, and I think I began to hate him, persuaded myself I would have looked after you better, understood you better... And then when Riffy was born it was like she was mine. I loved her so much, do love her—you will let me see her sometimes?' he asked quickly, as though she were about to refuse.

'Yes, of course. She loves you too. You are her godfather.'

'Yes. Thank you.' Searching Brogan's unhappy face, he sighed, continued determinedly, 'I've been doing a lot of thinking this last week, talking things over with Amanda. She was as horrified as my parents... And I went back to the hospital. I'd been having funny little pains in my legs—pins and needles—and I was scared witless, Brogan! I thought it meant something awful, and it didn't. They're going to be all right. Oh, Brogan, they're going to be all right.'

'I'm glad.'

'It will take a while—physio and everything— but...' Taking another deep breath, he asked softly, 'Will you forgive me?'

'Oh, Daniel!' she exclaimed helplessly. 'Yes, I forgive you. We were both victims of circumstance.'

'And you will come and see me sometimes? Bring Riffy? Let me come and see you?'

'Yes, of course.'

'I won't be a nuisance. Amanda and I—well, I quite like Amanda,' he blurted out awkwardly, and for the first time in a while she smiled.

'Good. Does Amanda like you?'

He gave a sheepish grin, nodded, then sobered. 'Joshua came to see me. We had a long talk. Oh, Brogan, won't you even see him?'

'No.'

'He's hurting.'

'Is he?' she asked with the semblance of indifference. But she wasn't indifferent, and she was hurting too. 'And he must have talked very well for you to become his champion.'

'Don't be bitter. Did you like him so very much?'

Turning away so that he wouldn't see her face, she grabbed the kettle and filled it. Like him? *Like?* Was it only liking when your bones melted at even the mention of his name?

'I've decided to move,' she stated abruptly. 'Live nearer a town. I'm a bit isolated here on my own.'

He sighed. 'If you need any help. I mean, if there's anything I can do...'

'No,' she said gently. There was nothing anyone could do.

'I'll clear out the annexe. Amanda's waiting outside in the van—she'll help. You won't move without telling me, will you?' he asked urgently.

'No.'

It took most of the afternoon to clear the annexe, and when they'd gone, when Riffy was in bed she stared out over the fields from her bedroom window, wondered if she'd been too precipitate. But

Joshua really hadn't seemed the sort of man to want a widow with a young baby. Not for keeps. And she needed it to be for keeps.

She'd been vaguely aware for some moments of the clatter of a helicopter overhead and hadn't paid it much attention, but as the noise grew louder, as the tops of the trees edging the field began to bend and sway she looked up.

Police, she supposed, or air force, except it was red and she didn't think either of those services used red helicopters. It was like a large red dragonfly, she thought absently, and watched without interest as it hovered over the cornfield then moved off to one side. And if it didn't go away it was going to wake Riffy. Tutting crossly, she turned away. Dennis the farmer wasn't going to be too happy if his corn got flattened.

Carefully opening the nursery door, she peeped inside, then walked across to the cot, a soft smile on her face. Riffy was lying on her back, covers kicked off, arms wide, little face serene, and she felt such a rush of love for this little scrap, this adorable, funny little daughter of hers that she wanted to pick her up, hold her warm body close, be comforted. She felt so *empty*—and became aware of silence. Thank goodness.

Hands on the end rail, she continued to stare at her daughter, think her own thoughts. They were muddled mostly, disconnected—vague plans about moving, where to go. And she sensed rather than heard someone behind her.

Whirling round, she stared at Joshua. Unsmiling, calm, inscrutable, he stood in the doorway, hands in his trouser pockets, legs braced, back straight, hair untidy, and the pain was—enormous.

'Helicopter,' she said stupidly.

'Mmm. Show-off?' he asked quietly. 'I didn't think, until too late, that I might wake Riffy. A bit difficult to land. Telephone wires,' he explained laconically.

'Yes.'

Glancing past her, he stared at her sleeping daughter, gave a faint smile, returned his gaze to Brogan. 'You look terrible,' he commented softly.

'Thank you.'

Searching her face, taking his time, he finally asked, 'Going to forgive me?'

She didn't answer, couldn't answer, didn't know what to say. Looking away, she walked across to the window and straightened a curtain that didn't need straightening.

His voice still soft, conversational, he added, 'I've had a hellish week.'

Have you? she thought. Have you? Want to know what mine's been like?

'Brogan?'

Resting her face against the window-frame, she closed her eyes in defeat, felt him move, heard quiet footsteps behind her, held her breath. He touched her shoulders, making her stiffen, slowly turned her, stared down into her averted face. 'I'm in love with you.'

She closed her eyes tighter, sucked in another breath.

'Oh, Brogan. Brogan, Brogan,' he sighed. Drawing her gently against him, he held her close, rested his chin on her head. 'Are you crying inside? Aching? Are you praying I will go away—or praying I will take it all out of your hands?

'I feel every bit as desperate as Daniel ever was. I feel empty and hurting and stupid, and angry. Dear God, have I been angry. I have an enormous house, an empty house, a very sad and lonely house—and I've been every bit as foolish as Daniel,' he added softly. 'I've bought a rocking-horse—the biggest, most glossy rocking-horse you've ever seen. And a teddy. Boy, is that one big teddy—'

'You don't like her,' she wailed.

'Like her? I *adore* her!'

'You don't,' she grizzled. 'You never laughed at her faces, kissed her, hugged her.'

'I didn't dare. I didn't want to be ensared. She would have been too easy to fall in love with. Do you know how *hard* it was not to laugh? I could have loved her the first moment I saw her.'

'But not her mother.'

'*Always* her mother.' Still holding her to him, he began rubbing one palm up and down her back—a comfort, a promise. 'Won't you even look at me, Brogan?'

She shook her head, stayed burrowed against him.

'Won't you allow me to love you?'

Snapping her head back, she stared into his face. 'Allow?' she choked. '*Allow?* You *know* how I feel!'

'Yes. But will you allow yourself to feel that way?'

'I don't *know*!' she exclaimed with soft ferocity. 'I don't know what you *want*!'

'You,' he said simply.

'You don't *know* me.'

'No, only how you make me feel.'

'But why?' she whispered helplessly.

'Why? I don't know *why*. Only that I do.'

'For an affair? A diversion? An apology? Out of *pity*? Guilt?'

'No. For always.' And he said it with such simplicity, so believingly that she was silenced. Momentarily, anyway.

'Always?' she echoed.

'Mmm. You, me, Riffy. I want her underfoot, in my arms. I want to see her funny faces, her smile, receive her kisses. And I want her mother to love me.'

Feeling tearful again, choked, she whispered helplessly, 'But you don't *know* me.'

'And does not knowing *me* make any difference to how you feel?'

Looking down, she shook her head.

'I've never seen the laughing, happy girl that people talk about—'

'People,' she scoffed half-heartedly. 'Daniel isn't "people".'

'No, but your friends in the village are.'

'I don't have many friends. I don't have time.'

'Yes, you do. You might not know it, but you're well liked, well thought of.'

'Blamed,' she said softly.

'No,' he denied gently. 'That's only in your mind. You were the only one who blamed you for the ac-

cident. I want to be loved, Brogan,' he added softly.
'I want to be loved by you.'

'You have *lots* of women! Daniel said so.'

'And none of them made me feel like this. None
of them made me feel I might be wanted. None of
them made me feel I could be loved.'

Staring into his eyes—eyes that showed no expression—she finally understood. Those dark, dark
eyes which she had once thought cold were not cold
but used very effectively as a shutter to hide his
thoughts, his emotions.

'Smile with your eyes,' she ordered abruptly, and
he blinked, looked surprised, then did so, and allowed them to crinkle at the corners, his mouth to
turn up in a smile. Rueful, wry, but extraordinarily
appealing.

'Better?' he asked with soft mockery. 'Now you.'

But she couldn't; suddenly, she couldn't. 'Oh,
damn you,' she cried, her eyes flooding with tears.
'Damn you.' Arms snaking round him, she held him
tight, buried her face once more in his shirt, and
cried—cried out all the dammed-up misery and
pain—and he held her, rocked her gently, soothed
her, waited patiently until the last hiccuping sob,
and then he raised her face, dried her tears with his
thumbs, and kissed her—softly, gently, on her
mouth, her eyelids, her tear-stained cheeks.

'Come,' he said softly. 'We don't want to wake
Riffy.'

She allowed herself to be led, one strong arm
round her waist, waiting whilst he closed the door
quietly behind them. He opened her bedroom door,
ushered her inside, left the door wide. Sitting her

on the edge of the bed, he reached for the box of tissues on the dressing table, handed them to her, then sat beside her whilst she blew her nose and composed herself.

'Better?'

'Yes. Sorry.'

Removing the box before she mangled it completely, tossing it onto the floor, he pulled her back into his arms.

'I want to kiss you,' he said softly, and pain lurched inside her, tangled in her stomach. Heat rose to her face as he gently turned her, stared at her parted lips, then slowly lowered his mouth to hers. Such a soft, gentle kiss, it was exploratory, devastatingly arousing, and one hand slid to his shoulder, the other round his back whilst his own palms framed her face, held it gently whilst he tasted every centimetre of her lower lip, then the upper.

Eyes closing, she gave herself up to pure seduction, pure bliss, pure excitement, as it curled in her stomach, ached in her groin, tightened her thighs until kissing was no longer enough.

Opening her eyes, she stared at him. He looked solemnly back.

'Don't be afraid to touch me, Brogan. Please don't. I need to be touched.' Taking her hand, he held it gently to his cheek, then turned his mouth and kissed the palm. 'Touch me. Even if it's only to hit me.'

She could feel the tension in him—the urgency, the stillness. 'I touched you before...' she began.

'And I rejected you. You can't forget? Forgive?'

'If you're lying...'

'I'm not lying.'

'Pretending...'

'Not pretending. I need you very badly, Brogan.'

But she couldn't get out of her head the fear that
in a few weeks, months he would grow cold again,
turn from her, say it was over. Yet all of life was
a gamble, wasn't it? And if she threw this away
now...

Her sigh shuddery, watching him very carefully,
she moved her hand to his strong, hard thigh, felt
the powerful muscles bunch, pulled his shirt from
his trousers so that her fingers could touch warm
flesh, and he groaned deep in his throat, laid her
gently back across the bed.

'Are you watching for a flicker of uncertainty?'
he asked softly. 'A hint of acting? Will you examine
everything I say for the trace of a lie? Do you think
yourself so very unlovable?'

She shook her head.

'Then let me love you,' he pleaded thickly. 'Let
me *love* you. Let me explore every exquisite inch
of you, touch you, hold you, excite you.'

Feeling her limbs grow heavy, she stared dazedly
into eyes that were almost black, felt helpless, mesmerised, sucked in a sharp breath when one palm
roved down over her breast, lingered, tightened.

'No lies, no rejection, no—uncertainty. I want
you as my wife, want Riffy as my daughter, and if
you say I must wait then I will wait. If you say no—
I will die.'

'Oh, Joshua,' she pleaded, 'I can't say no. You
know how you make me feel. And I don't want to
wait. I *can't* wait.' Her body had anticipated too

much already. And she knew very well that his had. With a shaking hand, she reached up, brushed his thick hair off his forehead. 'Love me,' she whispered huskily. 'Love me well, and please, dear God, don't ever hurt me again.'

His breath a hard lump in his chest, his own hand shaking, he slid his palm down to the hem of her skirt, raised it slowly—frustratingly slowly—as his eyes continued to stare into hers. She shuddered when his hand reached the line of her panties, groaned when his thumb probed, and could then take no more. With an inarticulate cry, she reached for him, helped him strip, helped him help her, and naked they moved higher on the bed, held each other tight.

To feel the heat of a man's naked body against her own, to feel his desire, his need, to be able to touch, trail her tongue across heated flesh, to feel again that odd restriction of ribs as though they were bound in iron, that spiral of painful desire with a man who could excite, a mouth that not only promised but gave enchantment—all the things she had ever yearned for, all the feelings that had needed release were made real, were given—and it went on for such a long time. Such a blissfully long time. Feverish, excited, yearning, she touched and touched again, as though she would never get enough of the feel of him, the taste of him, the strength of him, and it was beautiful, and fulfilling, and moreish.

'Dear God,' he whispered shakily as he lay spent beside her, one arm across her waist, the other hanging limply over the side of the bed. 'Dear God.'

Equally spent, astonished, and suddenly quite horrified at the extent of her passion, she peeked at him sideways, eyes wary.

He watched her, gave an odd little snort of laughter. 'That was a surprise...'

'Yes. I think... I don't... I'm sorry, I must have—'.

'Sorry?' he exclaimed, laughing. 'You're *apologising*? Oh, Brogan.' Hugging her against him, he kissed her, hard. 'I might have to go on a survival course, but don't, for goodness' sake, apologise.'

'It must have been building up,' she said weakly.

His lips twitched. 'Yes, I guess it must.'

'I've never... I mean, I always wanted, but...' That hint of uncertainty still at the back of her lovely eyes, she blurted out, 'Shall you mind? I mean, I don't think I'm a nyphomaniac or anything... Stop *laughing*!'

Face buried in the pillow, his voice muffled and uneven, he muttered, 'Oh, Brogan. I adore you.' Emerging slowly, tousled and appealing, he grinned at her, emotion no longer hidden, thoughts no longer hidden, eyes, in fact, full of warm laughter. 'Let's get married tomorrow. Let's get married tonight. Oh, Brogan, let's get married. I want to buy you the moon.'

'I wanted chocolates.'

'What?' Hoisting himself upright, he leaned over her. 'What?'

'I wanted chocolates,' she repeated. 'You bought me flowers and perfume and fruit and I was waiting for chocolates.'

'You mean that's all it would have taken?' he exclaimed. 'I went through *agonies*—dehydration, rejection—and all it would have taken was *chocolates*?'

'Yes. I like chocolate.'

His mouth twitched again, his eyes laughed. 'You wretch. Oh, you wretch.' The laugh in his eyes warming to a smile, his face gentling, he promised softly, 'Then chocolates you shall have. Along with anything else your heart desires. If it exists, then it's yours. But you have to marry me first,' he warned.

'I'll marry you first,' she said quickly, 'before you change your mind.'

'I won't,' he promised. 'You think that, having found you, I'm going to let you go?' He shook his head, smiled. 'Not ever.'

'Can Riffy be a bridesmaid?'

'Mmm. What will the elephant wear?'

She blinked, stared, and her smile started slowly, then widened, and then she laughed in delight as she pictured Riffy and elephant in matching frilly dresses. 'Oh, Joshua, yes! It would make everyone laugh. It'll be such a *happy* day!'

'And all the days to come,' he promised softly.

and

HARLEQUIN®

I N T R I G U E ®

Double Dare ya!

Identical twin authors Patricia Ryan and
Pamela Burford bring you a dynamic duo of
books that just happen to feature identical twins.

Meet Emma, the shy one, and her diva double,
Zara. Be prepared for twice the pleasure and
twice the excitement as they give two
unsuspecting men trouble times two!

In April, the scorching **Harlequin Temptation** novel
#631 **Twice the Spice** by Patricia Ryan

In May, the suspenseful **Harlequin Intrigue** novel
#420 **Twice Burned** by Pamela Burford

Pick up both—if you dare....

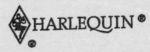

Look us up on-line at: http://www.romance.net   TWIN

MILLION DOLLAR SWEEPSTAKES
OFFICIAL RULES
NO PURCHASE NECESSARY TO ENTER

1. To enter, follow the directions published. Method of entry may vary. For eligibility, entries must be received no later than March 31, 1998. No liability is assumed for printing errors, lost, late, non-delivered or misdirected entries.

   To determine winners, the sweepstakes numbers assigned to submitted entries will be compared against a list of randomly, preselected prize winning numbers. In the event all prizes are not claimed via the return of prize winning numbers, random drawings will be held from among all other entries received to award unclaimed prizes.

2. Prize winners will be determined no later than June 30, 1998. Selection of winning numbers and random drawings are under the supervision of D. L. Blair, Inc., an independent judging organization whose decisions are final. Limit: one prize to a family or organization. No substitution will be made for any prize, except as offered. Taxes and duties on all prizes are the sole responsibility of winners. Winners will be notified by mail. Odds of winning are determined by the number of eligible entries distributed and received.

3. Sweepstakes open to residents of the U.S. (except Puerto Rico), Canada and Europe who are 18 years of age or older, except employees and immediate family members of Torstar Corp., D. L. Blair, Inc., their affiliates, subsidiaries, and all other agencies, entities, and persons connected with the use, marketing or conduct of this sweepstakes. All applicable laws and regulations apply. Sweepstakes offer void wherever prohibited by law. Any litigation within the province of Quebec respecting the conduct and awarding of a prize in this sweepstakes must be submitted to the Régie des alcools, des courses et des jeux. In order to win a prize, residents of Canada will be required to correctly answer a time-limited arithmetical skill-testing question to be administered by mail.

4. Winners of major prizes (Grand through Fourth) will be obligated to sign and return an Affidavit of Eligibility and Release of Liability within 30 days of notification. In the event of non-compliance within this time period or if a prize is returned as undeliverable, D. L. Blair, Inc. may at its sole discretion, award that prize to an alternate winner. By acceptance of their prize, winners consent to use of their names, photographs or other likeness for purposes of advertising, trade and promotion on behalf of Torstar Corp., its affiliates and subsidiaries, without further compensation unless prohibited by law. Torstar Corp. and D. L. Blair, Inc., their affiliates and subsidiaries are not responsible for errors in printing of sweepstakes and prize winning numbers. In the event a duplication of a prize winning number occurs, a random drawing will be held from among all entries received with that prize winning number to award that prize.

5. This sweepstakes is presented by Torstar Corp., its subsidiaries and affiliates in conjunction with book, merchandise and/or product offerings. The number of prizes to be awarded and their value are as follows: Grand Prize — $1,000,000 (payable at $33,333.33 a year for 30 years); First Prize — $50,000; Second Prize — $10,000; Third Prize — $5,000; 3 Fourth Prizes — $1,000 each; 10 Fifth Prizes — $250 each; 1,000 Sixth Prizes — $10 each. Values of all prizes are in U.S. currency. Prizes in each level will be presented in different creative executions, including various currencies, vehicles, merchandise and travel. Any presentation of a prize level in a currency other than U.S. currency represents an approximate equivalent to the U.S. currency prize for that level, at that time. Prize winners will have the opportunity of selecting any prize offered for that level; however, the actual non U.S. currency equivalent prize if offered and selected, shall be awarded at the exchange rate existing at 3:00 P.M. New York time on March 31, 1998. A travel prize option, if offered and selected by winner, must be completed within 12 months of selection and is subject to: traveling companion(s) completing and returning of a Release of Liability prior to travel; and hotel and flight accommodations availability. For a current list of all prize options offered within prize levels, send a self-addressed, stamped envelope (WA residents need not affix postage) to: MILLION DOLLAR SWEEPSTAKES Prize Options, P.O. Box 4456, Blair, NE 68009-4456, USA.

6. For a list of prize winners (available after July 31, 1998) send a separate, stamped, self-addressed envelope to: MILLION DOLLAR SWEEPSTAKES Winners, P.O. Box 4459, Blair, NE 68009-4459, USA.

Free Gift Offer

With a Free Gift proof-of-purchase
from any Harlequin® book, you can receive
a beautiful cubic zirconia pendant.

This stunning marquise-shaped stone is a genuine cubic
zirconia—accented by an 18" gold tone necklace.
(Approximate retail value $19.95)

Send for yours today...
compliments of ⬥HARLEQUIN®

To receive your free gift, a cubic zirconia pendant, send us one original proof-of-purchase, photocopies not accepted, from the back of any Harlequin Romance®, Harlequin Presents®, Harlequin Temptation®, Harlequin Superromance®, Harlequin Intrigue®, Harlequin American Romance®, or Harlequin Historicals® title available in February, March or April at your favorite retail outlet, together with the Free Gift Certificate, plus a check or money order for $1.65 U.S./$2.15 CAN. (do not send cash) to cover postage and handling, payable to Harlequin Free Gift Offer. We will send you the specified gift. Allow 6 to 8 weeks for delivery. Offer good until April 30, 1997, or while quantities last. Offer valid in the U.S. and Canada only.

Free Gift Certificate

Name: _____

Address: _____

City: _____ State/Province: _____ Zip/Postal Code: _____

Mail this certificate, one proof-of-purchase and a check or money order for postage and handling to: HARLEQUIN FREE GIFT OFFER 1997. In the U.S.: 3010 Walden Avenue, P.O. Box 9071, Buffalo NY 14269-9057. In Canada: P.O. Box 604, Fort Erie, Ontario L2Z 5X3.

FREE GIFT OFFER   084-KEZ

ONE PROOF-OF-PURCHASE

To collect your fabulous FREE GIFT, a cubic zirconia pendant, you must include this original proof-of-purchase for each gift with the properly completed Free Gift Certificate.

084-KEZ

HARLEQUIN ROMANCE'S 40TH ANNIVERSARY SWEEPSTAKES
OFFICIAL RULES—NO PURCHASE NECESSARY

To enter, complete an Official Entry Form or 3" x 5" card by hand printing the words "Harlequin Romance's 40th Anniversary Sweepstakes," your name and address thereon and mailing it to: In the U.S., Harlequin Romance's 40th Anniversary Sweepstakes, P.O. Box 9076, Buffalo, NY 14269-9076, or in Canada to Harlequin Romance's 40th Anniversary Sweepstakes, P.O. Box 637, Fort Erie, Ontario L2A 5X3. Limit: one entry per envelope, one prize to an individual, family or organization. Entries must be sent via first-class mail and be received no later than 7/31/97. No liability is assumed for lost, late or misdirected mail.

Prizes: 150 autographed hardbound books (value $9.95 each U.S./$11.98 each CAN.). Winners will be selected in a random drawing (to be conducted no later than 8/29/97) from among all eligible entries received by D. L. Blair, Inc., an independent judging organization whose decisions are final.

IF YOU HAVE INCLUDED THREE HARLEQUIN PROOFS OF PURCHASE PLUS APPROPRIATE SHIPPING AND HANDLING ($1.99 U.S. OR $2.99 CAN.) WITH YOUR ENTRY, YOU WILL RECEIVE A NONAUTOGRAPHED 40TH ANNIVERSARY COLLECTOR'S EDITION BOOK.

Sweepstakes offer is open only to residents of the U.S. (except Puerto Rico) and Canada who are 18 years of age or older, except employees and immediate family members of Harlequin Enterprises, Ltd., their affiliates, subsidiaries, and all other agencies, entities and persons connected with the use, marketing or conduct of this sweepstakes. All federal, state, provincial, municipal and local laws apply. Offer void wherever prohibited by law. Taxes and/or duties on prizes are the sole responsibility of the winners. Any litigation within the province of Quebec respecting the conduct and awarding of a prize in this sweepstakes may be submitted to the Régie des alcools, des courses et des jeux. All prizes will be awarded; winners will be notified by mail. No substitution for prizes is permitted. Odds of winning are dependent upon the number of eligible entries received.

Any prize or prize notification returned as undeliverable may result in the awarding of that prize to an alternative winner. By acceptance of their prize, winners consent to use of their names, photographs or likenesses for purposes of advertising, trade and promotion on behalf of Harlequin Enterprises, Ltd., without further compensation unless prohibited by law. In order to win a prize, residents of Canada will be required to correctly answer a time-limited, arithmetical skill-testing question administered by mail.

For a list of winners (available after September 30, 1997) send a separate stamped, self-addressed envelope to: Harlequin Romance's 40th Anniversary Sweepstakes Winners, P.O. Box 4200, Blair, NE 68009-4200, U.S.A.

HR40RULES

Happy Birthday to

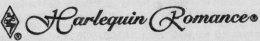 *Harlequin Romance*®

With the purchase of three Harlequin Romance books, you can send in for a FREE hardbound collector's edition and automatically enter Harlequin Romance's 40th Anniversary Sweepstakes.

FREE COLLECTOR'S EDITION BOOK

On the official entry form/proof-of-purchase coupon below, fill in your name, address and zip or postal code, and send it, plus $1.99 U.S./$2.99 CAN. for postage and handling (check or money order—please do not send cash), payable to Harlequin Books, to: In the U.S.: 3010 Walden Avenue, P.O. Box 9071, Buffalo, N.Y. 14269-9071; In Canada: P.O. Box 622, Fort Erie, Ontario L2A 5X3. Please allow 4-6 weeks for delivery. Order your FREE Collector's Edition now; quantities are limited. Offer for the free hardbound book expires December 31, 1997. Entries for the Specially Autographed 40th Anniversary Collector's Edition draw will be accepted only until July 31, 1997.

WIN A SPECIALLY AUTOGRAPHED COLLECTOR'S EDITION BOOK

To enter Harlequin Romance's 40th Anniversary Sweepstakes only, hand print on a 3" x 5" card the words "Harlequin Romance's 40th Anniversary Sweepstakes," your name and address and mail to: "40th Anniversary Harlequin Romance Sweepstakes"—in the U.S., 3010 Walden Avenue, P.O. Box 9076, Buffalo, N.Y. 14269-9076; in Canada, P.O. Box 637, Fort Erie, Ontario L2A 5X3. No purchase or obligation necessary to enter. Limit: one entry per envelope. Entries must be sent via first-class mail and be received no later than July 31, 1997. See back-page ad for complete sweepstakes rules.

Happy Birthday, Harlequin Romance!

Official Entry Form/Proof of Purchase

"Please send me my FREE
40th Anniversary Collector's Edition book and enter me in
Harlequin Romance's 40th Anniversary Sweepstakes."

Name: _____

Address: _____

City: _____

State/Prov.: _____ Zip/Postal Code: _____

089-KEP

089-KEP